# ONE HUNDRED DECISIONS

---

## AN ASPEN COVE SMALL TOWN ROMANCE

### KELLY COLLINS

BOOK NOOK PRESS

# CHAPTER ONE

Glancing around the office, Natalie took in the austere atmosphere. It looked more abandoned than the orphans who came through the door. The cracked linoleum and soiled white walls spoke more of despair than hope. It was almost as if the room knew the children passing through could end up in far worse situations than anyone could imagine.

Natalie Keane chewed the last bit of her thumbnail down to the quick. Her nerves were raw, and her insides shook. The last time she'd been in a room like this, she was six, her mother was dead, and they told her she had a new family. The social worker announced it in a way that sounded like she was getting a new pair of shoes.

"Ms. Keane, are you ready to meet your brother?"

Natalie's heart raced to fight or take flight. She'd been in Los Angeles for weeks, jumping through hoops to save a boy she'd never met. Was she ready? Hell no. She didn't do commitments, and becoming a guardian for her brother was a six-year gig. If she said yes, she had to be all in.

A thunderous beat boomed inside her chest before her heart stilled. "I still can't believe I have a brother." Until everything checked out, they had kept her away from him. "No use giving the boy false hope," they told her.

Mrs. Todd, a Los Angeles County social worker, nodded. "It was hard for Will to believe too. If there wasn't a written will, we would have never found you."

"I'm surprised you did; shocked, really. I've moved around a lot. And ... my father abandoned me over twenty years ago. Hard to believe he even remembered who I was." She rubbed her eyes. "Hard to comprehend that a man who discarded his family started a new one years later."

The situation still shook Natalie. Was it really two weeks ago that she had gotten the call? *Ms. Keane ... this is Roberta Todd from Los Angeles County, and we have your brother. You're listed as the chosen guardian. If you don't come to claim him, we'll have to find him a suitable home.*

Right then, it wouldn't have mattered if Will was her brother or not. At the mention of foster care, she would have gone to get the boy, regardless. As a product of the system, she knew there was a range to what they considered suitable care.

"It wasn't easy. We moved through the records by your name, then the driver's license number, and finally, your social security number to find you. It's always better to place a child with a responsible relative if possible."

Natalie's head felt like it was spinning. "How do you know I'm even his sister, or that I'm responsible? And where were you when my mother killed herself? Where was my father?"

Mrs. Todd frowned. "Thankfully, we have a more

2

connected society. Two decades ago, we didn't have the resources we do now to locate a person." She looked at her desk, where Will's file sat. "Honestly, you were probably better off not being with your father. By the looks of it, he wouldn't get a parent of the year award. You can say no. There's no shame in knowing your limitations."

She shook her head. "No, I'd never abandon him."

"Let me get him."

Mrs. Todd walked out the door, giving Natalie more time to think. She had no idea how she would support a preteen boy. She could barely make ends meet herself, but there was no way she'd leave him here to face who knows what.

*Do or die; I'll try.* She repeated the mantra that got her through the worst of times.

The door opened and in walked a lanky kid dressed in tattered jeans and a Harry Potter T-shirt. His hair was too long, and his suspicious eyes told her he'd already seen too much in his twelve years, but she couldn't deny he was her brother. Looking at him was like looking at herself more than a decade and a half before.

Sadly, as she was gaining her freedom from the system, poor Will was being born and raised to live in it.

Natalie approached him with the same reserve. She grabbed courage from some hidden resources inside and said, "Hi, I'm Natalie. You must be Will." She held out her hand.

He looked at her open palm and stepped back.

"Will," Mrs. Todd scolded. "This is your sister who drove all the way from Colorado. Don't you think she deserves more—maybe a hello?"

For a long moment, he studied her. "Sorry. Hi." He shoved his hands into his jean pockets and stared at the floor. "I don't know why I can't stay in the house. It's not like my father was around, anyway. I can take care of myself."

"The house didn't belong to your father. It was a rental, and we can't set a twelve-year-old free to care for himself," Mrs. Todd answered. "It's your sister or back to the center until we can find you a home."

Natalie's heart ached for him. At twelve, she'd thought she could care for herself too. She ran away from her third foster care family and hid in a treehouse in the next town over. All it took was the pangs of hunger a day later to bring her home. Turned out, her foster family hadn't even realized she'd left. She'd learned then that she was worthless in their eyes, and several foster families later proved her assumption was right. They never wanted her, just the money they got for taking her in.

Looking at Will tugged at her heart, which was odd because emotional attachment wasn't a strength for her. Not that she couldn't love—it was that she didn't trust love. She hoped he was only looking for stability. At this point, it was all she could offer.

"How about we try it," Natalie said. "I passed their tests, took their classes, and filled out the paperwork. We can leave for Colorado now." Her shoulders raised in a shrug. "Sometimes, a new beginning can change your world."

He lifted his head to look at her, and he rolled his eyes. "Colorado might as well be a different world. What about my friends?"

Natalie imagined he didn't have many, if any. Kids like him were never part of the in-crowd. They were the outliers who walked on the fringe of society. "You can call them, or maybe they can visit you in Aspen Cove."

Will let out an exasperated exhale. "Whatever." He looked around the room. When his eyes lit on the backpack in the corner, he rushed to pick it up.

"Is that all you have?" Natalie stared at the blue backpack with alarm. There couldn't have been more than one change of clothes inside.

Her finances were already tight, with only a little wiggle room for extras.

"Hold on." Mrs. Todd went to her filing cabinet and pulled out a Visa gift card. "We have a donor that sends a few of these a year for kids who really need it. I'd say Will could use a few extra items." She held the card in the air. "Here's two hundred and fifty dollars for clothes and necessities." She eyed Will. "That doesn't include toys or video games. Got it?"

"We'll see." He rose up to swipe it, but Mrs. Todd was quicker than Will and handed the card to Natalie, who took it and put it straight into her bag.

"Necessities mean necessary," the social worker said.

Will groaned. "Ugh."

Mrs. Todd walked them to the door. "We have notified Colorado Social Services of the transfer, and they will be in touch."

Natalie wasn't sure what "be in touch" meant. She knew they'd eventually do a home visit and check on the welfare of her new ward. If it was anything like when she grew up, Will might be in college before they got around to it. She wasn't against the system that saved many children. With anything in the world, there was a failure rate, and she had fallen in that small percentage.

"You ready?" she asked.

He stood tall and stiffened his shoulders. Despite his tough exterior, she could see the indecision in his cautious green eyes. Rather than stand his ground, he followed her. No doubt because his options were limited, and sadly she was the best one he had. They walked past Mrs. Todd and out the door into the overcast day.

"Take care, Will. Good luck, Natalie." Mrs. Todd gave them a wave before she went back inside.

"What kind of car do you have?" he asked.

"Who said I had a car?" she teased. "Maybe I have a horse. Or … maybe we're hitchhiking." She held up her thumb.

He stopped and narrowed his eyes. "Are you sure you're my sister? They could have duped you into taking me."

She led him to the parking lot toward the beat-up green Subaru.

"Nope, I'm not sure, but they said I was, and I'm inclined to believe them. We could take a DNA test, but if you're Gerald Palmer's son, then I'm confident we're related." She opened the door and climbed behind the steering wheel. "Besides, we look similar."

"I look nothing like you. You're a chick." Will stood at the front of the car as if debating to get inside or bolt.

She pulled the door shut and rolled down the window. "You're observant, and I'm starving. How about In-N-Out?"

His eyes grew wide, and the tiniest of smiles lifted his lips. He raced to the passenger side and hopped into the front seat.

"Are you rich?"

She laughed so hard she snorted. "No, I barely keep myself above the poverty level."

"Great, so nothing will change."

She turned to face him. "Listen, Will, I don't know

what your life was like, but I'm guessing it wasn't all that great." She heaved a sigh. "All I can promise is a place to live, a full stomach, and an ear when you need one. Living with me will not be rainbows and unicorns, but it keeps you out of the foster care system." She started the car and backed out of the parking spot. "Let me tell you, you don't want to be a ward of California. I've been there, and sometimes it's not pretty."

He buckled in and turned his head to face her. "Why didn't you grow up with me?"

She took a left and drove across the street to In-N-Out. It was a splurge, but all new experiences should start right, and a burger and fries seemed perfect.

"Our dad left my mom, and she died a short time later. His name wasn't on the birth certificate, and no one knew to look for him."

She placed their order and pulled around to the window to pay.

"Were they married?"

She shook her head. "Nope. What about your parents?" She paid for their meal and took the bag. The car filled with the smell of fresh fries and grilled burgers. To a twelve-year-old growing boy, it must have smelled like heaven.

"Same, although my mom didn't die. She was a stripper, and she didn't want a kid. I don't even know her name." He dug into the bag and took out his meal.

*Karma is a bitch.* It seemed fitting for Gerald to get saddled with a kid when he'd done the same to her mom. The bastard walked out one day, and he never came back.

She reached inside the bag and pulled out a few fries. They were a perfect amount of fat and salt to make a girl swoon. "These are so good." She dipped her hand back into the white paper sack to get a few more. "There isn't an In-N-Out where I live, but I hear they're building one in Denver soon." She turned onto the street that led to the freeway. If she got on the road now, they could make it most of the way to Colorado that day.

"How far is it to Denver?"

"From home or from here?"

"Both," Will spoke with his mouth full.

She'd have to correct that habit. Bad manners weren't a character defect, and changing them was possible, but now wasn't the time.

"We've got a twenty-plus hour drive to Aspen Cove. From there, Denver is another couple of hours." She pulled her hamburger out of the bag and unwrapped enough to take a bite.

"So, basically, you live in the middle of nowhere."

She swallowed. "It's somewhere. Give it a chance; you might like it."

"Does it have an arcade?"

She turned onto the highway heading north. "No."

"Skateboard park?"

She shook her head. "No. Do you ride a skateboard?" She could put that on the wishing wall at B's Bakery and hope someone had one they weren't using.

"No, just wondering. What does it have?"

Thinking about Aspen Cove made her smile. "It has nice people."

"Basically, you're moving me to hell."

She glanced at him quickly enough to see a frown, but she didn't reply.

They drove the next six hours in silence. When her tank teetered on empty, she pulled into the truck stop and gassed up.

"If you need to go to the restroom, do it now. I'm not a fan of rest stops. They aren't safe for women or children."

Will dragged his feet toward the store while she filled up the Subaru. When she finished, she walked inside. In the third aisle, she found Will shoving a candy bar into his front pocket.

"Ready?" she asked.

He jumped back and looked around. They walked toward the door, but she moved to the right and stopped at the register. Reaching for a pack of gum, she smiled at the cashier. "I'll take this, and my brother has a candy bar in his pocket." She stared at Will. "Give it to him so the man can ring us up."

Will opened and closed his mouth a few times before he tugged the bar of chocolate free and slapped it on the counter with a huff.

Once she paid, and they were back inside the car, she gripped the steering wheel tightly, then turned her head toward him.

"It's time to lay down some rules. We're family, and that means I've got your back. I saved you from foster care, but I can't save you from yourself, and I won't visit you in jail. I don't know what Gerald allowed or expected, but from this point forward, you don't steal. Got it? We have just enough money to live on. I can't afford a lawyer to represent you when you get arrested. If you want or need something, you ask for it or work for it."

He buckled his seatbelt and crossed his arms. "You got any more rules for me?"

"Probably, but we can make them up as we go. I've never been a big sister, and I don't know how this family stuff works. I'm flying by the seat of my pants here. Don't make it harder."

He growled. "I really am in hell."

She pulled out of the parking lot and headed north-east. "No, hell is moving from home to home because no one wants you. Or their lives are more messed up than yours, and they can't keep you. It's sleeping three to a bed and eating a meal a day until the social worker comes. It's being punished in a way that doesn't show the bruises. I came for you because I want you to have better."

"You don't even know me. I could be a serial killer. Hell, you could be one."

She laughed. "Statistically, serial killers are middle-aged white men. I think we're both safe. I know more about you than you think. At twelve, you've probably had more adult responsibilities than most adults. You steal what you can't buy. You're used to having little, but you crave something more. Am I close?"

He twisted in his seat and leaned his head against the window. "You're right about one thing—I want more."

She reached over and ruffled his hair. "Well, I'm more."

"How much longer do we have?"

"Forever. We can stop at a motel, we can't afford, to rest, or we can push through and make the trip on caffeine and adrenaline, and then crawl into bed when we get home. What do you think?"

He shrugged. "Let's go home."

IN THE EARLY hours of the morning, she pulled into her driveway. The sound of gravel crunching under the tires was all she could hear. Her tiny house was a sight to see. It wasn't much, but it was home.

Will woke and rubbed the sleep from his eyes. "Are we here?" He leaned forward and looked at the wooden box in front of them.

It was eight feet wide and twenty-five feet long for a whopping two hundred square feet of living space. Basically, she lived in a furnished storage container.

"Yes, this is home—for now."

There was no way she could live in a shoebox with a growing boy long-term, but this was what she could afford, and it would have to do. Moving wasn't in the budget. The trip had eaten up her emergency fund. All she had was forty dollars for food, and the gift card she would use to buy Will clothes.

His jaw dropped. "You said this would be more. Where's the house?"

"This is the house."

"What the hell, Natalie? This is like living in a cardboard box behind a dumpster."

"You might be right about the box, but I take offense to the dumpster. Now come inside. I need a few hours of sleep before my shift tomorrow." Thankfully, she'd called Maisey from the road and was told she could return right away.

Will grabbed his backpack and followed her into the house. "I suppose it's better than the place they had me in the last few weeks." He scanned the room and plopped onto the loveseat in the living room. "It was basically a homeless shelter for kids." He hugged his backpack to his chest. "I walked in there with more, but someone stole my stuff."

She shrugged off her sweater and hung it on the hook by the door. "How did that feel?"

He eyed her, knowing where she was going with the question. "It felt like shit."

"Language, mister. You're twelve. Act like it. As for the theft, it sucks, but maybe it's karma for all the stuff you've stolen."

"How would you know?"

She pointed to the loft. "I was you nearly two decades ago. Now get to bed. You can take the loft, and I'll take the couch." She gave him her bed for two reasons. The first being he was too tall for the love seat, and the second because he'd have to make it past her to leave.

"What will I do while you're at work?" He trudged to the ladder and pulled himself up, rung by rung.

"You'll have to come with me until I figure out another plan."

"I can take care of myself."

"So you've said." She pulled a blanket from the box next to the couch. It served as a table and storage. "Let's try something different. How about I care for you for a while? You be a kid, and I'll be the grown-up." The words sounded great. Hopefully, she wouldn't be another disappointment in his life.

"Grown-up people live in houses."

"This is a house. It's efficient. Grow up and deal with it."

He peeked over the side of the loft and laughed. "You just told me to be a kid."

"You can start tomorrow." Exhausted from the trip, she collapsed on the cushions and pulled the blanket over her worn-out body. "Good night, Will. I promise everything will be all right." She turned out the light and prayed she wasn't lying.

# CHAPTER TWO

Jake Powers stood in front of the store he would open today. He didn't understand why there was a need for the cloak and dagger routine, but Doc Parker thought it would be nice to treat the residents of Aspen Cove to a surprise.

As he looked at the covered sign and windows, he almost agreed. It was fun keeping things under wraps. Kind of like a Christmas present under the tree waiting to be opened.

A quote came to mind. *Life is not what happens to you, but how you deal with what happens to you.*

That was how he'd ended up in Aspen Cove.

He checked his phone for the time and found he had a good forty minutes before the grand opening. That was enough time to eat.

Following the scent of bacon, he moved down Main Street toward Maisey's Diner. The bell above the door rang as he entered.

The booths held the usual crowd. Two of the town's firemen sat at a front booth by the window.

"Morning." Jake waved as he walked by.

"Big day for you—for us," Luke said. He was one of only a few people who knew what was replacing the old Dry Goods Store since he had to make sure the building was up to fire code standards.

"Definitely. I hope the residents like it as much as Doc thinks they will. Maybe I should have opened an ice cream store instead."

Thomas frowned. "It's not an ice cream shop?" He raised his hand and pretended to check off an item from an invisible list. "That was Eden's guess. That or a candy store. You know, the kind with a taffy pulling machine in the window."

"It's not that either," Jake said as he took the corner booth beside them. He looked around the diner for Maisey, Riley, or Louise. They'd been serving him for weeks and knew his dietary restrictions. "Who's on shift today?"

Thomas looked over his shoulder to answer. "Natalie. She's old." He shook his head. "Not old as in age, but she's worked here for a while. She left for a bit. You'll like her. She's sweet."

"Hopefully, she's fast, or I'll be late to the grand reveal."

The swinging door to the kitchen opened and out walked a cute brunette. Her eyes scanned the room and settled on a boy slumped in the corner. She set a plate of pancakes in front of him, and he perked up.

Jake couldn't hear the exchange, but by the frown on the kid's face, it didn't look pleasant.

She spun around, and in seconds, she stood before him. "Good morning. I'm Natalie. Can I get you coffee to start?"

"Orange juice, please, and a glass of water." He took her in from the high ponytail to her Keds. His eyes moved up to linger for a few seconds on pink lips that looked pillow-soft. But it was her eyes that really drew him in; green eyes with dark circles beneath them that spoke of exhaustion.

"Only juice and water?" she asked again.

"No, I'm eating too, but I'm in a bit of a hurry. Can you put my order in right away?"

"Sure thing." She reached into her pocket for her pad. "What can I get you?"

"Bacon and eggs, over medium, please. Tell them it's for Jake, and they'll know how I like it."

She scribbled something on the pad and walked away. He watched the sexy sway of her hips until she got to the window and slapped the paper to the wheel, spinning it around. "Order in," she called. Seconds later, she made the coffee rounds, filling up cup after cup of Maisey's brew. Coffee was one thing he missed. Giving it up was part of his healthier lifestyle.

While he waited, he went through his email messages. As a life coach, he got a lot of them. Life shouldn't be so complicated, but many people found it impossible to tackle, and that's where he came in. Perspective was his business. He had a talent for looking at the big picture and breaking it down into reasonable bites.

Ten minutes later, Natalie swung by and dropped off his plate without stopping. He knew right away that it was all wrong. The bacon wasn't his bacon—turkey bacon. It was the thick-cut strips cooked perfectly to a crisp. Years ago, he would have gobbled down two orders, but things were different now.

With limited time, he couldn't wait for another order, so he pushed the bacon aside and started on the eggs. The first bite hit his tongue, and the salt nearly choked him. He reached for the water, but she hadn't brought it or the juice.

He raised his hand to flag down the waitress. "Excuse me," came out in a garble. Several heads turned, including Natalie's.

Rushing over, she asked, "Is something wrong?"

He let go of an exasperated breath and forced himself to swallow the bite stuck in his throat.

"This has salt. I asked for no salt."

She shook her head. "No, you didn't."

"Putting Jake at the top of the order is the same."

She took the ticket from her pocket and frowned. "Jake means no salt?"

"Yes. Are you trying to kill me?"

She gave him an eye roll worthy of an award. "Hardly. If I had murder on my mind, I wouldn't do it with salt when I hear arsenic works much quicker."

He shoved the plate away. "How about I make it easy on you? I'll have dry white toast and the orange juice I ordered, but you never brought." He raised a brow in annoyance. "If it's not too much trouble," he added with a hint of sarcasm. "I need it to go."

She spun around and left without a word. He wouldn't call her sweet, but she was cute.

When she came back five minutes later, she set a paper bag and cup on the table. "Here you go. Toast and juice on the house. I'd hate for you to ruin Maisey's Diner's reputation when the error was mine."

He appreciated that she took responsibility because few people did these days.

"I'd never say a bad word about the diner or Maisey. She's been kind since my arrival."

Natalie eyed him with curiosity. "Are you a new resident of Aspen Cove?"

"No, just paying a debt, and then I'm gone."

He scooted out of the booth and stood beside her. He wouldn't consider himself a tall man at five foot ten and standing next to her, his chin aligned with the top of her head. "Are you coming to the grand opening?"

"Nope, I'm working." She peeked over her shoulder. "I've got rent to pay and a boy to feed."

He peeked back to the kid eating pancakes in the corner and nodded before he made his way out of the diner and down the street. He slipped past the growing crowd and into the shop. The thought of a crowd in Aspen Cove made him chuckle. While the population was on the upturn, Doc told him he estimated it to be about a thousand. In Phoenix, that was the line at his favorite tea shop on any day. Or so it felt.

A double knock followed by three more was the agreed-upon signal. When Jake heard Doc pound out the rhythm on the front door, he put his uneaten toast under the counter and headed outside.

"Hello," he said to the dozen people standing in front of the store. Looking out, he recognized many of the faces. Katie from B's Bakery was there, as was her husband, Bowie. Sage and Cannon stood beside them. Thomas held his son Tommy in one arm and wrapped his other around his wife, Eden. Agatha was nearby with the edge of a sheet in her hand that was attached to the sign cover. Doc stood back and smiled.

Jake wondered if the store was for the community or Doc. He seemed to take great pleasure in the process.

"So glad you could make it." Jake looked up at the cloth-covered sign. "There's been a lot of speculation about what was happening inside. I've heard ideas like an ice cream parlor and a candy shop floating around, but sadly, that's not where this is headed. However, this place will nourish your mind and soul." He looked at Agatha and nodded.

With a big tug, she pulled the edge of the fabric, and the sign for B's Book Nook swung in the breeze.

A collective gasp came from the growing crowd, followed by shouts of glee.

"Come on in, and I'll tell you how this came about." He led them into the bookstore and stepped onto a stool, then began to speak. "My name is Jake Powers, and Bea Bennett saved my life." He pointed to the pink letter now framed at the entrance. "Over ten years ago, I suffered kidney failure. I spent many days and hours hooked up to a dialysis machine. My life looked grim from where I sat in the cold, sterile room of the renal health center. That was until Bea Bennett did the unthinkable. In her time of complete loss and devastation, she donated her daughter's organs."

The room, once filled with hushed chatter, went silent, and several heads turned to look at Bowie, who nodded and smiled. He wrapped his arm around Katie and pulled her closer to his side.

"I understand that Brandy's death affected many people in this town. It profoundly affected me. The gift was a near-perfect match."

Doc cleared his throat. "Some of you might wonder why it took him ten years." He looked at Jake. "Get on with it, son. There are so many books and so little time."

"To expedite this, all I will say is donor lists, including

donor and recipients, are confidential, but Bea somehow broke the system and found me, and here I am. I'll never be able to bring Brandy back, but I heard she loved books. So, in a roundabout way, this is her gift to you but given through me. B's Book Nook is named for both mother and daughter. You can't buy happiness, but you can buy books, and that's kind of the same thing. This shop is a non-profit venture, and we will discount books by twenty-five percent at the register. Enjoy." He stepped off the stool and walked toward Bowie. "Can I talk to you for a minute?"

While everyone moved through the stacks, he and Bowie took a seat at a table in the corner.

The shop was filled with the scent of paper, glue, and excitement.

"I know the sacrifice was yours, too," he said to Bowie. Doc had told him how Brandy had been Bowie's fiancée. "I'm sorry for your loss."

Bowie smiled. "Funny how things work out, right? Brandy's death was torture, but it was also salvation. Without it, I wouldn't have Katie, who is also a recipient of Bea and Brandy's gift. Without Katie, I wouldn't have my daughter Sahara." He rubbed his chin. "Thank you for wanting to give back." He looked around the bookstore and smiled. "Brandy would have loved this. And Bea ..." He shrugged. "Put a section of Agatha Christie books in the corner, and you wouldn't have gotten her to leave."

"I've got Agatha tucked into the mystery section." He pointed to the Harry Potter book display. "Maybe we'll dedicate next week to Hercule Poirot and Miss Marple."

"Sounds like you might be a bibliophile yourself."

"Not much to do during treatments but read."

Bowie gripped the edge of the table and rose. "Will

KELLY COLLINS

you stay in Aspen Cove?" He chuckled and shook his head. "I know it sounds awful, and I'm not making light of the situation, but it seems as if Brandy is returning to town one organ at a time."

Jake's eyes grew wide. "It's a great place to be, but it's not where my life is." He rarely told people what he did because there were so many questions that followed. "I'm a coach of sorts."

"I know who you are." He tapped his shirt pocket where the outline of his phone showed. "I googled you. Just figured you could practice what you preach: 'Enjoy your life. The finish line comes far too fast.'"

Jake stood and shook Bowie's hand. "Maybe you should be a life coach."

"Just repeating your wisdom. All I want to be is a good man, a good husband, and a good father. If I can do that ... I'm a total success."

As Bowie walked away, Jake thought of the ways to measure success. His measurement had always been counting the people he'd helped. But was that truly a measure of his success, or his ability to help others triumph?

As he watched the townsfolk move around the store, he considered the focus of their lives. They were generous. Considerate. Compassionate. He was certain the people of Aspen Cove would make anyone feel like they belonged. He shook the thoughts from his head. He was here to repay a kindness. His future had a different path. If all went well, he'd be moving to Los Angeles to partner with Vision Quest, an exclusive retreat center for high-profile clients. All he needed to do was to seal the deal and hire someone to take over the bookstore. It couldn't be that difficult, could it?

# CHAPTER THREE

"Where did everyone go?" Natalie leaned on the counter and stared at the empty tables and booths. The only person seated was Will, and that was because she didn't want him to get into trouble, so she fed him and let him play games on her phone.

Ben walked from the kitchen into the diner to get a soda. "Big opening today."

"I heard, but what opened that caused a mass exodus?" She glanced at the clock on the wall. It was almost noon, and the place was silent. No customers meant no tips.

"Bowie texted and said it's a bookstore."

Will's head snapped up from the phone. "Did you say there was a bookstore?" He slid from the booth and nearly ran to where she stood. "Can we go?" He clapped his hands together and bounced on the balls of his feet. "Please." He looked from her to Ben as if hoping one of them would say yes.

Ben swiped a napkin from the holder on the countertop and wiped the sweat from his brow. "Who's this lad?" Ben asked.

Will shuffled his feet and danced back and forth. Maybe feeding him a double stack of chocolate chip pancakes wasn't a wise move.

"This ball of energy is my brother, Will." It sounded weird when she said it. Brother meant family, and family meant love. Tired and scared was how she felt right now.

Ben's eyes grew wide. "Didn't know you had a brother."

"Neither did I."

"There's a story there."

"Yep, but I'm too tired to tell it."

Ben looked around the empty diner. "I think I've got this. Why don't you take the boy to the bookstore? There are worse things he could be excited about."

Will threw a celebratory fist into the air. "Yeah, sis, I'm not knocking up a girl or streamlining heroin."

"It's mainlining, and I'll ignore the girl comment." She hadn't considered Will could be sexually active at twelve. A twinge of anxiety fisted her heart. She was woefully unprepared to raise a boy entering puberty. "You and I will have a talk."

"I already know about the birds and the bees. The bigger question is, how do you know about heroin?" His eyes dimmed before her as if the light lit by the possibility of visiting the bookstore was put out by a flood of concern. Will was so young, but his eyes were those of an old soul.

"I read and, apparently, so do you. Let's go."

There was no need to ask twice. Getting Will to the bookstore was far easier than the job of getting him out of bed that morning.

They left the diner and walked to where the old Dry

Goods Store used to be. Above the door, hanging from a wrought iron arm, was a wooden sign that swung in the breeze.

"Who's B?" Will asked.

"I never met her, but she used to live here, and by the way people describe her, she was a modern-day Mother Teresa."

"Who is Mother Teresa?"

She gripped the fancy brass handle of the door and pulled it open. "I thought you read."

"I do, but I read good stuff like *Ender's Game* and *Harry Potter*."

Inside, the room smelled like a public library minus the sour scent of unbathed homeless men. She knew that smell well. Like Will, she'd escaped her misery by climbing inside the bindings of books. She spent hours reading and rereading classics like *National Velvet*, *Gone with the Wind*, and *Pride and Prejudice*.

As she glanced around the shop, she knew why the diner was empty. A person could spend days in a place like this and not see everything.

Abby Garrett sat at a table with a stack of books on horticulture and bees. Sage and Cannon stood at the counter, paying for their treasures. Agatha manned the old-fashioned register, the kind that sat like a golden trophy on the end of the counter, with its fancy gold fili-gree scrollwork and shiny black keys. The sound of the bell when the drawer opened, transported Natalie to a time long ago when women carried parasols and men wore holsters. This store could have risen from the pages of a *Little House on the Prairie* book with its antique register and hardwood shelves. Stepping into B's Book Nook was like entering a story—one from an era where mothers didn't commit suicide and fathers didn't overdose.

Will dashed off to a collection of Harry Potter books on display while she moved toward a pink sheet of paper framed and hung by the door. Behind the glass was a letter.

*Dear Recipient,*

*I know it's unusual for a donor's family to reach out to the beneficiary, but I wanted you to know a little about your gift giver.*

*They kept the registry private and if this letter found you, it means I hired the right person for the job. A good PI is like a good bra. It's working behind the scene, but it's holding up its end of the bargain. To track you down could be considered intrusive, but on some level, you became family the moment the gift was received.*

*I thought I'd let you know a little about Brandy. She was warm sunshine on a cold winter's day, a flicker of light in a dark moment, and as sweet as Abby's honey.*

*She was adopted, but somehow, I knew she was born to be mine. Brandy lived fully, loved deeply, and laughed heartily. While she was taken far too soon, knowing she lives in others makes the loss bearable.*

*My hope is that her sweetness flows through you. Smile more than you frown, laugh more than you cry, and give more than you take. Most importantly, have a long and fruitful life.*

*With love,*

*Bea*

"Did you come here to finish the job?" A deep voice sounded from behind her. She pivoted around to face Jake.

"I'm fresh out of arsenic." Her eyes went back to the framed page. "Are you this person?"

"I'm not Bea Bennett." He glanced down at his pants. "Anatomically impossible."

She let out a half sigh, half growl. "I meant the recipient?"

He nodded. "Yes, I have one of Brandy's kidneys."

"And the bookstore is your way of giving back?"

"Hardly seems equivalent. She saved my life, and I financed a bookstore. Not that big of a deal."

She moved to the side, reaching out to touch the spines of the books that filled the nearby shelves. "Oh, I don't know. Reading books lets you experience thousands of lifetimes. They can transport you to any time and place, or you can become any character in a story. Today I might be Peter Pan and tomorrow a muggle named Hermione."

"Very true. Or you could be Natalie, a woman who probably wouldn't have gotten my order wrong if she wasn't so tired."

She rubbed at her eyes. "Is it that obvious?"

"Probably not to most, but my job is people-centric, so I notice things that others might not."

She looked toward the door. "Speaking of jobs, I better get back to mine. It's lunchtime, and I can't expect Ben to run the place alone."

She glanced up at him and saw the fine lines that etched the corners of his eyes when he smiled. Those thoughtful and expressive eyes saw more than she wanted to expose.

She tore her gaze away and shook her head. "Sorry, I was just ..." She almost told him she was drowning in the depth of his blue eyes. "I've got to go."

He chuckled. "Have a good day, Natalie."

"You too." She searched the aisles for Will and found him at the Harry Potter display.

"Can I get these?" he asked.

They were hardback books that no doubt included a hefty price tag. "Sorry, bud, but those are out of the budget."

His eyes turned accusatory. "You've got a preloaded credit card with two hundred and fifty dollars on it."

"That's for necessities like clothes." She reached into her front pocket and pulled out ten wrinkled one-dollar bills. "This is your book budget. On my day off, we can go to Copper Creek and get a library card so you can borrow the other books you want to read but can't afford."

He stomped his foot. "I hate being poor."

"There are worse things."

"Like what?" he snapped back.

"Being homeless, hungry, or dead." *Or lonely.* She turned to leave and found Jake staring at her as if he'd heard her thoughts. "Be back at the diner in fifteen minutes," she told Will.

Will walked away and disappeared down an aisle.

As she moved toward the door, she considered saying goodbye to Jake, but Agatha pulled him behind the counter to ask questions, so she left without a word.

When she got back to Maisey's, she found poor Ben running around like a headless chicken. Book shopping created an appetite.

Riley, Maisey's niece, was tying on a spare apron just as she rounded the counter.

"I've got it. I guess I lost track of time."

"Let me help you get caught up, and then I'll go." Riley still pulled shifts at the diner even though she made

26

thousands on her metal art sculptures. Not that she needed the money, but it was a way to show her loyalty to her Aunt Maisey.

"I appreciate it." They moved around each other getting the drinks delivered and the orders placed to the growing crowd. If this was any other town than Aspen Cove, Natalie would have bet a busload of starving tourists had been let loose in front of the diner.

Between orders, Riley talked about her newest project —a flock of life-sized peacocks for some Denver eccentric's front yard. Average people stuck pink flamingos on wire legs into their lawns, but this guy wanted peacocks made of bronze, and Riley was happy to make them for thousands of dollars each.

Oh, to have a different skill set than waiting tables. A girl could dream, and then she had to get real. Schlepping plates paid the bills.

During a lull, they stood behind the counter and took a breath while Riley waited for Ben to make her lunch.

"Anything new at the Guild Creative Center?" Natalie had been there once when Poppy Dawson got married to Deputy Sheriff Mark Bancroft. Poppy's photography was on display as a tribute to the people of Aspen Cove. That was the last time she'd visited the building.

"It's been quiet. Dalton's always there cooking something. Samantha comes and goes depending on if she's touring or not. She's back in town prepping for the summer concert and recording a new album. I imagine her band will show up soon."

"What about that painter?" The woman who came out of the womb with a paintbrush and palette in her hand had always intrigued her.

"Sosie Grant?" Riley lifted her hands into the air. "She used to come here on weekends, but she hasn't been around for months." She shrugged. "Maybe her muse is sleeping, and she's taking a break. I once took a year off because I wasn't feeling creative." She poured herself a soda. "Or maybe it was because I burned down my workspace. Either way, sometimes, life happens."

"Order up," Ben called from the window.

"That's mine." Riley glanced around the diner. "You got it from here?" She snatched the plate filled with a burger and fries from the shelf.

"Yep, thanks for your help."

The crowd arrived together and left together, which meant she was stuck clearing off at least a dozen tables.

When the bell above the door rang, she looked up to see Jake and Will. How had she forgotten about her brother?

"Oh my God, I'm so sorry."

"Babysitting is not really my thing."

She fisted her hips and glared at Will. "I said fifteen minutes." She turned back to Jake. "I really told him to be back in fifteen minutes."

"I lost track of time." Will ambled toward the booth in the corner. The frayed ends of his jeans swept the floor as he walked.

*That kid needs some clothes. Clothes that fit.*

"He's back now. Do you think you can put in an order that won't send me into kidney failure?"

His smile was disarming, but she wasn't sure if it was authentic or there to hide his jibe.

"What's your poison?" She pulled her order pad from her pocket and, in big letters at the top of the ticket, she wrote JAKE and turned it to show him.

"Grilled chicken breast and veggies."

She cocked her head to the side. "Ben can make stuff that's not dipped in batter and fried to a crisp?"

"So it would seem."

After a quick look at Will, she turned back to Jake. There was something about him that pulled and pushed at her. It wasn't his strong jaw, or his sea-glass blue eyes that seemed to look through her; not his height or his broad shoulders. All she knew was that she wanted to like him and dislike him at the same time.

"If you need to get back to the store, I can send Will to deliver the order."

He smiled wide enough to show his pearly whites. Perfect teeth that any dentist would be proud to slap on an advertisement.

"That would be great. I need to get up a help wanted sign and start next week's order. Who knew this town had so many readers?"

"Who said we could read?" She turned and walked away.

From the door, he called, "Not what I meant."

"But it's what you implied." She didn't know why his statement riled her.

Twenty minutes later, Will delivered the meal. When he returned, he tucked himself into the booth again. Only this time, he sat reading *Harry Potter and the Chamber of Secrets*.

"How could you afford that?" she asked.

"Grand Opening. Everything was half-price."

# CHAPTER FOUR

Jake sipped his coffee and walked around the bookstore. He had to admit giving this community the gift of words made his heart swell with pride. Doc was right. He used a line from the movie *Field of Dreams*, "If you build it, they will come." And they did. Tiny spaces of emptiness dotted the shelves where tightly packed books had been yesterday.

He turned at the sound of the door opening behind him to find Agatha. She shuffled inside and tucked her bag under the counter.

"Good morning, Agatha. Looks like we got off to a good start yesterday."

"I'd say it was a home run."

He found it funny how both she and Doc used baseball references when referring to the Book Nook.

"If I can find someone to take over running the place, I'd call it a complete success."

Agatha plopped on the stool behind the register. "You've done a fine job." She pointed to the framed stationery. "I didn't know Bea, but from what I hear, she

30

would have been proud. Too bad you can't stay and run it. You've been here a bit and fit right in."

He chuckled. "I wouldn't say I fit in. I feel like a square block shoved into a circular hole, but my edges are wearing down, and the fit gets easier each day." This whole adventure had been an experience for him, from staying at Tilden Cool's efficiency cabin to eating most of his meals in the diner. In his experience, most small communities were guarded with strangers, but not the people of Aspen Cove. They were the poster children for hospitality.

"Maybe you should stay." She lifted her brows to nearly touch her curled white hair. "Who knows, maybe the other kidney will come home too." She looked around as if making sure no one but him could hear. "I mean, her heart is here already. If Bea contacted all the organ recipients, I'm told there's another kidney, a liver, a pair of lungs, and some corneas walking around."

It painted a funny picture in his mind of organs bouncing into town on their own.

"I couldn't say, but if there are more pink letters, I'd brace myself for visits. Nothing deserves a thank you like the gift of life."

She thunked her travel mug on the counter. "Do you want to go over the sales for yesterday, so we know what to order?" she asked.

He imagined stocking a bookstore wasn't the same as the pharmacy where she worked with Doc. There was more to it than filling a space. Some books would always sell. Popular tomes like *Game of Thrones* would be staples, as would romance novels, cozy mysteries, and the New York Times top one hundred, but books were very much like produce. Their shelf life was limited, and a fresh supply of new titles needed stocking with regularity.

"I see you sold a Harry Potter book. We'll need to replace that." JK Rowling had burst onto the scene with book one over two decades ago, and it was still going strong. That was the staying power he wanted with his business. His goal was to be a household name like Tony Robbins.

"I didn't sell it," she said. "You must have sold it after I left."

He rubbed his chin, brushing against the scruff he'd adopted since his arrival. "Nope, Frank Arden came in for the latest Grisham book, and a schoolteacher bought every Shel Silverstein book we had."

"That must have been Mercy Meyer from Rose Lane. Did Peter Larkin from over there on Pansy come in?"

"He did. How did you know?"

She shook her head. "He said he would visit and ask you to stock *Playboy* since we don't sell it at the pharmacy."

Calling it a pharmacy was a stretch since he couldn't get a prescription refill. All Doc stocked was over the counter and pharmaceutical samples.

"I gave him the bad news, no *Playboy* here, but he purchased our only copy of the *Kama Sutra*." He looked around the display for the missing Harry Potter novel. It was there before Natalie's son came in to bring his dinner.

"I'll let Doc know to stock up on ace bandages and ibuprofen for when Peter strains a muscle," Agatha said.

The old man was a marvel. If rumors were true, he saw more action than the newlyweds in town. After a thorough look for the missing book, he came up empty-handed. He hated to accuse someone of theft, but Will had been looking at them earlier that afternoon. In fact, he'd dog-eared a page in the missing book, which was why he'd brought him back to the diner. It was fine to read the books, but dogearing a novel was considered literary abuse by many.

"Hey, Agatha, I need to go to the diner. Can you hold down the fort for a bit?"

"You going to see that pretty little waitress, Natalie?" Her eyes sparkled with mischief. "She'd be perfect for you."

"I am." He walked out the door with two questions on his mind. First, was Natalie's son a thief? Second, why did most women north of fifty consider themselves match-makers? He needed a woman less than he needed a kidney stone. But like a kidney stone, pretty women were hard to ignore.

The morning sun warmed his back as he walked to the diner. Back home in Phoenix, it would already be sweltering. By noon on a summer day, the temperatures would hit triple digits. That was another plus to the merger with Vision Quest. He'd have to move to California, where the weather was consistently perfect.

The bell above the door rang as he entered. The regular cast of characters was present. Doc sat at his booth in the right back corner, reading the paper. The fire department crew filled a booth at the window. Sheriff Cooper and his family sat at a table near the center of the room. At the counter was Peter Larkin. A few stools down was Baxter Black, the construction wizard who had done the remodel on the bookstore.

Natalie walked from behind the counter with a pot of coffee swinging between her fingers. "Morning, Jake."

It was nice she remembered his name, but then again, she got a lesson in writing it at the top of the order pad.

"Natalie." He nodded and moved to a booth against the left wall.

After she made her rounds, she stopped in front of him. "What can I kill you with today?" she teased. Her smile was like seeing a rainbow for the first time. He had a feeling not much made Natalie smile authentically, and he was happy she'd gifted him with one.

He'd seen her fake smile in action several times, but this was different. He hated that his purpose in coming might flip that smile into a frown.

"How about some tea and a bowl of oatmeal?"

She scrunched her nose. "Do you miss good food?"

He laughed. "I'd miss living more."

She tapped her pen on the table. "Good point. I'll be right back."

She returned moments later with a cup of hot water and a saucer that held an assortment of teas.

"Do you have a minute to talk?"

She looked over her shoulder. "Sure." She slid into the booth across from him. "What's on your mind?"

He wasn't sure how to start the conversation. He thought it best to ease into it. "You know the Book Nook probably won't ever be profitable, right?"

She stared at him with a blank expression. "I imagine it will be difficult given the population, but there are many tourists that visit for the fishing and hiking. Books on trails and popular local sites like the waterfalls might help revenue." She cocked her head to the side. "You didn't say that to get advice, right? Is there a reason you're telling me this?"

"Yes, the book prices are discounted, so the revenue

collected is enough to cover the essentials like stock, utilities, insurance, and salaries, but theft isn't something I expected. At least not so soon."

Her shoulders stiffened as if she already knew what he would say and had to brace herself for the hit.

"What are you getting at?"

"I think your son stole a book. Did he somehow have a copy of *Harry Potter and the Chamber of Secrets*?"

Her cheeks bloomed red. "I gave him money. He said he bought it."

He shook his head. "Nope. He never spent a dime. I think it happened when he delivered my dinner. I went into the back room to get my meds, and when I came out, he was gone. I wasn't paying much attention to the display, but it's missing and unaccounted for in the sales report. We use the old register for ambiance, but scan the books so we can keep track of price and inventory. It wasn't sold yesterday."

Natalie shrank into the booth. "I'm sorry. I'll pay for the book." She reached into her pocket and pulled out a wad of ones.

He shook his head. "I'm a strong believer in owning our mistakes. Don't you think Will should pay for it?"

An exasperated sigh had her shrinking another inch into the red pleather bench. "I just know he's a good kid. I feel it in my bones. His life hasn't been easy as far as I know, but I only just met him. Obviously, I need to have another talk about stealing."

There were two things that jumped out of her statement. The first was she didn't know Will well, which meant he wasn't her son. The second was this theft wasn't his first if she'd already had the talk about shoplifting.

"I'm sorry. I just assumed he was your kid. He resembles you a bit. Especially in the eyes."

"He's my brother. I just found out when social services called and said he needed a home because our father OD'd."

As a life coach, he'd dealt with everything from substance abuse to narcissism. "You share a father but didn't know about him?"

Her lips stretched into a thin line. "It's a long story." She looked toward the window where his oatmeal sat, probably cold by now. "Besides, your breakfast is ready." She moved to get up, and he reached out to take her hand. The light touch sent tendrils of heat up his arm. "Let's meet tomorrow and figure out how to deal with this. The debt is not yours; it's Will's. You should never rescue a kid from his failures. There are valuable lessons learned from them." He let her hand go and gone with it was the comfort of its warmth. "I'll figure out a way he can work it off."

She put on a fake smile and rushed to get his oatmeal. While he ate, he considered Natalie and Will. He didn't think they were residents of Aspen Cove. When people who lived here talked of others, they came with a street attached, like Mercy Meyer from Rose Lane or Peter Larkin over there on Pansy. When Natalie's name came up, it was just Natalie. Was this a stopping point on a bigger path for her or was landing here a safety net that caught her when she fell? He needed more information. It looked like he'd need to do a bit of private eye work himself. Who was Natalie, and why did it matter so much to him?

# CHAPTER FIVE

Natalie finished her shift and marched across the street to get Will from the fire station. Luke had been kind enough to let him hang out for a while, so the kid didn't die of boredom. When she entered the building, she saw him sitting in the driver's side of the rig.

"Time to go," she called out, waving him down.

Luke came around from the backside of the truck. "He's a good kid. I think we might have a fireman in the making."

She smiled. "That's a possibility if he lives long enough. Thanks for letting him hang out with you guys. Sitting in the diner's corner isn't much fun for a kid."

Will opened the door and hopped down, coming over to stand beside her.

"Thank Mr. Mosier for his hospitality." If there was one thing she would instill in her brother, it was manners. The world was full of rude people, and she refused to let Will be a part of that herd. She didn't have much, but she had good manners, and that went a long way in the world.

"You rock, Luke."

She slipped her hand around his arm and led him out of the firehouse. "You're in big trouble, young man."

He tugged away. "Why? Because I wouldn't call him Mr. Mosier? He'd already told me to call him Luke."

She took several deep breaths while they walked to her Subaru. "Just give me a few minutes to calm down. I'm so angry at you, I could scream."

He climbed inside the passenger seat and pressed his fingers to his temples. "Well, don't. I've got a headache."

"Yeah." She turned to glare at him. "I've got one too. It's a twelve-year-old problem."

She spent the twenty-minute drive home brooding. Life was tough, and now she had a preteen on her hands who was determined to make it worse. When she pulled onto the gravel driveway and parked in front of her home, she told him to meet her inside.

She stayed outside and tried to come up with a plan. He'd only been with her a few days and, in that time, he'd stolen two things. If she hadn't seen the candy bar, he would have gotten away with it. She was torn because Will's previous life hadn't been the best. With a loser of a father, he'd probably been programmed to steal to survive. Bad habits were hard to break, but this one had to go immediately.

She walked into the house and found him slumped on the couch, arms crossed, and lips pinched.

"This place sucks."

She glanced around. He was right. For a single person, it was fine, but put two in a tiny box, and there were bound to be problems. She sat down and pivoted her body, so she faced him.

"Yes, this sucks, but it's better than living on the street with a shopping cart for your belongings, and a cardboard box for your house." She shook as she took a breath. "And I'm certain it's superior to living in a cell with a roommate named Bubba, who has a thing for young boys."

"Is this how my summer will be? I want to go back to Los Angeles. At least there, I had shit to do."

"Language. Let your words show your intelligence, not your ignorance."

"Whatever." He tightened his arms across his chest.

She recognized the body language. It was as good as armor. She didn't know how to ease into the subject they had to discuss, so she blurted it out. "Jake knows you stole the book."

He reared up as if to bolt. "I told you I paid for it."

"Now you're lying, which is just as bad. I know you stole it because even half-priced, that book would have never been ten dollars."

He narrowed his eyes and fell back into the cushion. "This is your fault. You didn't give me enough money. What am I supposed to do all day? At least back home, there was a television when we had power."

"Are you listening to yourself?" She didn't mean to raise her voice, but it climbed at least a full octave. "There is no home in Los Angeles. Since this is our only house, you'll have to make do with what we have. And what we have is what I can afford. If you keep stealing, we'll have less because people don't like thieves and don't trust the families of thieves."

"I'm not a thief. I'm a borrower, and I would have returned it."

She closed her eyes and sighed. The breath came out

in a whoosh that puffed out her lips. "The Book Nook isn't a library. I told you I'd take you to Copper Creek. You stole that book. It doesn't matter if you had planned to return it or not. You took it without permission. Tomorrow, we're visiting Jake, and you'll apologize. He said he'd figure out a way to let you work off the debt."

"I'm not apologizing."

"Yes, you are. That's what civilized people do. They admit their mistakes and correct them."

He leaned in, so he was inches from her face. His cheeks turned red, verging on purple. "My biggest mistake was coming here to live with you."

His words sliced through her. The rusty edge of his sharp tongue cut into her soul. Maybe bringing him here had been a bad idea. She mentally reinforced the steel around her heart by reminding herself that no one wanted to be with her. It's why her father left early on. Why her mother checked out of life when she was six, and why her brother wanted to go back to the hellhole he came from.

"Stop being ungrateful."

They were more alike than she imagined. The only difference was she had learned to keep things inside; whereas, he was too immature to know how to compartmentalize and turn his emotions into little bombs that only detonated on occasion. Nope, Will was an open field of explosives. Too bad she didn't have the time or patience to tiptoe across his minefield.

"You don't know what it's like to be me," he yelled.

"Yes, I do. We have the same father, and it looks like he didn't change much."

Will jumped up and stomped outside. She didn't go after him because sometimes a person needed space. But when darkness blanketed the house, and he'd missed dinner, she started to worry. She kept telling herself she didn't care, but that was a lie.

When it inched toward ten o'clock, she considered calling the police. Maybe she should have done that first. She'd considered it, but fear kept her from dialing the number. All they needed was a police report connected to them, and he'd end up in the foster system—the one place she wanted him to avoid.

Given the situation, maybe she had been naïve to think he'd want to stay here with her. Not every foster family was bad. She'd had a few good ones in her time. They were generally the transition homes. The places she stayed before a more permanent solution was available. Those parents always seemed nice. Then again, they didn't have to invest much in the kids that blew through. Here today and gone tomorrow.

At fifteen minutes to eleven, she heard his shoes kick up the gravel. When the door opened, she didn't say a word.

He came in and sat next to her. Goose bumps prickled his skin, and tears stained his cheeks.

She took the blanket draped over the sofa and placed it around his shoulders. When he leaned into her, she stiffened but then relaxed. She wasn't getting soft. She was providing needed warmth. At least that's what she told herself.

"I thought you would want to be a family." The words stuck in her throat. "But if you think it would be better to live somewhere else, I'll call social services tomorrow. I only want what's best for you, Will."

He burrowed into her side as his body trembled. At first, she assumed he shook from the cold, but little hiccups broke through, and she realized he was crying.

"It's okay, Will."

"No, it's not," he cried. "I'm sorry, Natalie. I'm so sorry. I don't want you to give me away."

She held his shoulders and eased him back so he could see her face. She wanted him to look into her eyes and know the truth. "Maybe we're looking at this from the wrong angle. I'm not the enemy, and you're not the problem." She tugged him back to her chest. "Maybe you're a gift in disguise."

He sucked in a choppy breath. "Non-returnable."

She shook her head. "Nope. No returns." She held him until his sobs turned into whimpers and moved to an occasional out of sync breath. When she was certain he was calm, she said, "Let's set the ground rules again. This isn't me being a dictator. This is me trying to set a good example."

"I know. No lying. No stealing. No being disrespectful."

She smiled. "And no running away. There are bears in that forest. Wolves too." She looked down at the kid who, for the first time, resembled a twelve-year-old.

"You hungry?"

"Starving."

"Let's feed you, and then to bed. We need to get up early and head into Copper Creek for that library card and some clothes. You can't wear the same pants every day."

She rose from the couch and walked the few feet to the kitchen. "How about a sandwich? We've got peanut butter and jelly or bologna and cheese."

He rubbed his stomach. "Can I have both?"

She laughed. "You're going to eat me out of house and home, aren't you?"

He looked around the tiny place. "It wouldn't take much."

They stood side by side, making sandwiches. Something about the simple task made her heart hitch. For the first time in a long time, she didn't feel alone, and she wasn't sure if that was a good thing.

# CHAPTER SIX

Jake picked up his keys and walked out of the tiny cabin where he'd been staying.

Off to the right, Tilden was bent over planting flowers in the boxes surrounding the big house. He stood up. "I hear the opening went well."

Jake wanted to laugh. Great by Aspen Cove standards would be a failure by any other. He wasn't used to failing.

"Yes, the townsfolk seemed pleased with the idea."

"I'm glad you were the one who brought a bookstore to Aspen Cove. They had asked me a while back because I dabble in writing. For me, running a bookstore is on par with getting eaten by a bear. Not on my bucket list."

"It's not too bad, actually—running the bookstore, that is. It's kind of like working in a candy store." Jake looked up into the canopy of trees. "Will there be enough light to grow petunias?" He loved the colorful flowers but knew they needed sunshine to flourish. Every living thing needed something to flourish, whether it be respect, love, or space.

"Nope, I told Goldie, and she didn't listen. She

doesn't hear me when it's something she wants, and she wants petunias."

Goldie was the reason he was staying in Tilden's cabin in the first place. She'd been a social media maven and had her finger on the pulse of anything that was newsworthy. Apparently, she was a fan of his teachings.

"You know what they say ... happy wife equals a happy life."

"Anything that makes Goldie happy makes me happy," Tilden said.

"I heard that," she said, exiting the house with two cups of coffee in her hand. "And that makes me happy." She sidled up to Tilden and handed him a cup. "I guess you'll be leaving us soon, now that you've done your part."

He lifted a shoulder. "As soon as I find someone to manage the shop. What kind of benefactor would I be if I stayed open one day and then closed the place down the next?"

"You should think about staying long-term," Goldie said. "It's a great place to live, and that's coming from a girl who once lived in a penthouse and ate caviar for breakfast. Given the two lifestyles, I'd choose this one every single time."

"That's because of Tilden. Love blooms when you fertilize the heart with happiness, hope, and happily ever after."

Tilden drank his coffee. "Did you make that shit up on the fly?"

He laughed. "I did. It's my superpower."

Goldie huffed. "It's only super if it's relevant and powerful if you practice what you preach."

"I've got to go. I thought maybe I'd stop in at Maisey's for a stack of pancakes and a tea." He made his way to the rented SUV and turned to find Tilden and Goldie waving goodbye.

Just before he closed the door, he heard Goldie giggle and say, "Come on, Tilden, it's time to fertilize me with happiness."

He backed out and drove down the mountain road. The whole way into town, he thought about love and life, and what his happy ever after looked like. Fifteen years ago, it included marriage, and babies, and a home with a picket fence. Then, polycystic kidney disease happened.

He parked behind the bookstore and walked around to Maisey's. He expected to see Natalie when he entered, and he took a seat in a nearby booth, but she wasn't there. In her place was Maisey.

"Hey, handsome. Cakes, oatmeal, or eggs?"

"Pancakes today." He took another look around. "Is Natalie here?" For all he knew, she could have been in the back doing some kind of prep work.

"She's got the late shift because she needed to take Will into Copper Creek for clothes." She leaned a hip against the table. "Poor kid had the clothes on his back and a spare set in his bag. Can you imagine having so little?"

He couldn't. Not really. His life had been good. His parents had been solid. Though his family wasn't rich, they never wanted or needed for anything. Now that he was successful, they'd never need to ask for anything. He made sure his family was taken care of.

"What's the story with Natalie?"

"Let me get your tea and put your order in, then I'll join you."

She came back with two mugs, one filled with coffee

46

for her, and the other with hot water for him. She pulled his favorite decaf tea packet from the pocket of her apron.

"You wanted to talk about Natalie?"

He shook his head. "No, I don't want to talk about her. I want to know about her. What's her story?"

She leaned against the back of the booth and watched him like an experiment. "Don't you think you should ask her?"

"Probably, but she seems to have her hands full."

"That she does." Maisey leaned forward like she had a secret. "Poor kid gets a call that says she needs to pick up her brother, or he's going into foster care. She had no idea she had a brother. Imagine the fearlessness it takes to drive to California to pick up a kid she's never met. She's just a kid herself."

Natalie was young, but he wouldn't call her a kid. He imagined she was in her late twenties or early thirties. "That's a lot to take on. Does she have help? A boyfriend? A husband?" It sounded like he was digging for information.

"Nope, as far as I know, she's got no one. That was until Will. She's a hard worker. Not much of a sharer. What I've gathered I've pieced together from bits and pieces. From what she says, and the stuff she doesn't. I think she came here looking for something." She mindlessly folded a napkin and placed it under his mug. "I think she wants to belong, but she's afraid to take the leap. For as long as she's been here, Natalie has had one foot in Aspen Cove and the other out."

"Order up," Ben called from the kitchen.

"That's yours." She hopped up and got his breakfast. He sat in silence, thinking about Natalie and Will. Would he have been courageous enough to do the same? How many people would have driven across the country to pick up a kid they didn't know? That said something about her strength and tenacity. Two traits that had always been attractive to him.

When he got to the bookstore and opened the doors, a little pony-tailed girl trotted next to him. She looked up. "Hello, my name is Bailey Brown."

A woman in her thirties walked in after her. "Bailey, don't forget, you can have one book and don't put anything up your nose." She turned to Jake. "Hi. I'm Mallory Brown, and that little critter is my daughter." She looked around the store. "You don't have tiny candies or beans or pencils lying about, do you?"

He quickly deduced that Bailey liked to stick things where they didn't belong. "No." He gave her a quizzical look. "Pencils?"

She laughed. "That must have sounded crazy. A few months ago, she pulled the eraser off a pencil, and poor Dr. Lydia spent over an hour trying to get it out of her nose. Last month she got a bean stuck in her ear canal."

He chuckled. "No pencils that I know of, but there is a book with a box of beads attached." He leaned to the side to see past Mrs. Brown to Bailey. "Yep, looks like she found it."

"Oh no." Mrs. Brown took off at a sprint toward her daughter. "Bailey, you put that down, or I will thump you."

A minute later, Mrs. Brown had Bailey by the hand, leading her out the door empty-handed.

Agatha walked in around eleven. "Just checking on you. I can't help today. Doc and I are headed to Silver Springs to the movies." She smiled. "If he buys me dinner, he may get lucky tonight."

Jake's eyes opened wide. He didn't know how to respond to that. The only thing he knew was the geriatric residents of Aspen Cove saw more action than him. "Umm, have fun?"

"I see that look on your face. You young ones are impossible. Your mind went straight to the gutter when what I meant was, if Doc bought me dinner, he'd get lucky because I'd bake his favorite dessert."

"Sure, that's what you meant." He knew by the twinkle in her eye that she knew exactly what she was doing.

"You need to get some help in here. I'm too old to have two jobs."

He winked at her. "If you're still thinking about that kind of dessert, you're not old at all." Pointing to the help wanted sign he hung in the window, he said, "I'm working on it."

The door opened and in came Natalie and Will. Both looked as if they were walking the plank or heading to the scaffolds for a hanging.

Agatha glanced between them; her eyes focused on the book in Will's hand. "I better get going. Looks to me like you have an important meeting." Agatha might have been elderly, but she moved quickly when she wanted to, and she left the bookstore as quickly as an Olympic sprinter off the blocks.

He pointed to one of the tables in the shop. He'd had many shapes and sizes brought in, so people could sit and enjoy. He envisioned the Book Nook as a place where the residents gathered. Where people could play checkers and kids could do homework. He even considered selling coffee and tea, but liquids and books weren't a good mix.

"Hey, Will, I'm Jake."

The boy took a seat and hung his head. "I'm supposed to tell you I'm sorry."

He glanced at Natalie in time to see her roll her pretty eyes. Then he turned back to Will. "Are you sorry?"

Will traced the graphics on the cover. "Yes, I am."

"Good, because a sincere apology is the first step in making amends."

"I apologize, too," Natalie said. "I've never had a brother and never had kids. I didn't even babysit as a teen." The words spilled forth quickly. "Honestly, I don't know how to raise a twelve-year-old boy."

Jake sat back. "I hear it takes a village. Having been here a couple of weeks, I'd say Aspen Cove is the perfect place for Will to grow up. As for the book"—he shrugged —"like I told you yesterday, he can work off the debt. I've got stock to unpack. The restroom needs cleaning, and the floors could use a sweep."

"I'm not cleaning the bathroom," Will blurted.

They both glared at him.

"Fine," he grumbled. "But do I get to keep the book?"

Will seemed like the typical twelve-year-old with a one-track mind, but his eyes told another story. There was a lifetime of hurt and worry etched behind the green.

Natalie gripped the edge of the table and stood. "I've got to go. My shift starts soon." She nodded to Will. "It looks like yours does too."

A look of horror was in Will's eyes. "You're leaving me with him? He could be a serial killer."

"He's not."

"But he fits the profile. He's a middle-aged white man."

"I'm thirty-six. I'd hardly call that middle-aged."

Technically it was, but somehow the term didn't sit comfortably in his head.

"You're ancient," Will tossed back.

Natalie moved toward the door. "Promise not to kill him?"

His shoulders shook with his laughter. "That's a tough promise to make. What if I promise not to implicate you?"

Will waved his hand in the air. "I'm here, and I can hear you plan my death."

Jake rose from the table and walked Natalie the rest of the way to the door. "Would anyone miss him?" He stared at her lips as her tongue snuck out to lick the dryness away. A thread of heat uncoiled in his stomach and settled lower. What the hell was happening to him? He hadn't had that strong of a reaction to a woman in years.

She sidestepped him to look at her brother. A smile spread across her face. "I might miss him. The jury is still deliberating. Bring him back when he drives you crazy." She walked out.

Jake returned to the table. "Ready to earn your keep?"

# CHAPTER SEVEN

Natalie finished filling the salt and pepper shakers and turned around when the bell above the door rang. Jake walked in with Will, who looked tired but happy.

"Looks like you both survived." She glanced around the nearly empty diner. The only person present was Baxter, and he was finished. "Sit wherever you want."

As usual, Will trudged toward the corner booth. He seemed to like the out of the way space where he could go unnoticed and watch everyone. She would have picked the same table.

She'd learned to read people early on. It was an act of self-preservation.

Though it had only been a couple of days, she knew Will would want a root beer and guessed on tea for Jake.

She brought the drinks along with her and set them down on the chipped Formica tabletop. Reaching over, she ruffled Will's hair. "You hungry?"

"Starving." He looked at Jake and smiled. "He made me dust all the shelves, sweep the floor, stock and clean the bathroom. I oiled the furniture, washed the windows, and read."

"You read? How is that a chore?"

"Work hard and reap the rewards," Jake said. "Take shortcuts and deal with the consequences. He earned that reading time." When he looked at her and winked, her heart somersaulted and landed in her stomach. It wasn't a feeling she felt often. She likened it to having whipped cream with hot chocolate. The warm sugary sweetness tasted good despite not being good for her.

"What did you read?" He'd already nearly devoured the second Harry Potter book. That morning they'd driven into Copper Creek and bought him clothes. On the way back, they stopped by the library for a card and book three.

"*Hunger Games*," he said with excitement. "Jake said I could read it if I promised not to fold the corners of the pages." He drank his root beer and wiped the drop running down his chin with his sleeve.

"Hey, buddy, use your napkin. We just bought that shirt, and it needs to last."

He lowered his head. "Sucks to be poor."

"It's all perspective. There are people with less, and to them you're rich," Jake piped in. "I'd say you've got a pretty sweet deal going on here. You've got a sister who cares, you're fed, and you look healthy."

"Speaking of feeding—" She pulled out her notepad and looked at Jake. "I'm guessing grilled chicken and veggies for you." She turned to her brother. "Cheeseburger or fried chicken?"

"Burger."

"You got it." She scrawled Jake's name across the top while she walked to the window and clipped the order on the wheel. Next, she checked on Baxter. "Do you need a piece of pie, or anything else?"

"I need a good night's sleep," he said.

"You and me both." She rubbed her tired eyes. "I've been sleeping on the couch so Will could have the bed. It's not conducive to a good night's rest. Kind of lumpy and, every time I move, the frame squeaks."

"I won't complain then." He pushed his plate away. "My biggest problem is the smell of muffins coming through the floorboards. That and working on my house way too late into the night."

"You bought a house?" She hated when a prick of envy pierced her gut.

"Yep, it's a small two-bedroom bungalow on Hyacinth. It was the cheapest place in town because it had no roof. The plumbing and wiring are shot, but I'm working on it bit by bit. If all goes well, I should be out of the apartment above the bakery by late summer or early fall."

She leaned against the booth. "I don't know what I'll do. I wasn't expecting a roommate."

"Sometimes it's the unexpected that's the most rewarding." He looked toward Will and Jake. "He's your brother, right?"

"News travels fast."

"Small town living at its finest."

"True, but I love it." She stared out the window. "There's such a feeling of community here."

"There is. I'm fairly new in town, and yet I feel like I know everyone. Why don't you live in town?"

"I couldn't afford the rent. Besides, most of the places are falling down, and I don't have your skill set. I can paint and garden, but plumbing and electrical are beyond me."

"There's lots of development going on. Between that real estate mogul Mason Van der Veen and Wes, there's bound to be something opening soon. Aspen Cove is growing faster than California did during the gold rush."

She closed her eyes and imagined living in a house where she could spread her arms and turn around without hitting anything, a place where Will had his own room. Where the kitchen had full-sized appliances. A home with a shower that didn't share the same space as the toilet. The only benefit to that layout was she could sit to shave her legs.

"I hope Aspen Cove never loses its charm." Why she loved it, she couldn't say, but she was drawn to the tiny town.

"Everything changes, but who knows. Some change is good. Holy hell, we have a bookstore. That job was how I could afford the house. I'd call that a good thing."

"I'm happy for you." Even though she was envious, she was excited for Baxter. He was one of the good guys. All a person had to do was see him with his twin Riley to know they were nice people. He treated her like she mattered.

Baxter turned his head toward the corner table where Jake and Will sat talking. "Your brother seems to have found a friend in Jake."

"More of a mentor, I think."

"Order up," Ben called.

"You need anything else?"

"Nah, I'm good." He pulled a twenty from his pocket and placed it on the table. "Keep the change." He slid out of the booth and left.

She swiped up his dirty plate and the twenty and went to deliver her next order.

"Thank you," Jake said as she put his plate of chicken and steamed broccoli in front of him.

"You're welcome."

When she set the cheeseburger down for her brother, she reminded him not to waste.

"What about you? Have you eaten?" Jake asked.

"I'm good." She never liked to lie. She was starving, but her employee meal went to Will. Although Maisey probably wouldn't mind if she got something else, she never wanted to take advantage of someone's generosity. "I'll eat at home."

Jake eyed her, then nodded. "Are you off soon?"

How long had it been since she heard anything close to those words? Her last job was as a cocktail waitress in a dive bar in Taos. Nightly, she got a pat on the bottom and a "Hey, babe, what time do you get off?" Somehow, Jake's asking didn't seem to be a pick-up line. Although the way he constantly stared at her lips said otherwise. Not that she would have minded. Jake was right up her alley: sexy, nice, and temporary.

"I'm off at four. Riley is coming in to take over."

"How many days a week do you work?"

"Are you hitting on my sister?" Will asked.

Jake's cheeks turned pink. "No. Just ... just ..."

Will grabbed his stomach and fell onto the bench laughing.

"Ignore him." She turned her back on her brother. "I usually work six days a week, but two days are half shifts."

"Six days?" Jake asked.

"If I'm lucky. I like the work. It keeps me busy, and it's the only time I really socialize."

Will sat up. "Sounds like hell to me."

She frowned at him. "What did I tell you about your language?"

He lowered his head. "Let my words show my intelligence, not my ignorance."

"I'll have to write that one down," Jake said.

"Quote collector?" she asked.

"No. Life coach."

Will cocked his head. "People need coaches to live?"

"Some. I'm more of a mentor."

Natalie threw her fist into the air. "Nailed it."

"Nailed what?" asked Jake.

She shook her head. "Nothing." She turned to Will. "Eat up. Riley will be here in a few minutes, and we need to leave." She walked away, smiling. She'd never met a life coach, although she probably needed one. A coach who looked like Jake could be a bonus.

Fifteen minutes later, Riley walked in for her shift, and she and Will walked out. The entire twenty-minute drive home Will talked her ears off about the bookstore and Jake.

"Nat, he's the coolest guy. Did you know he's got some chick's kidney inside him?"

She'd never been given a nickname, and she liked it. "I did. You'll meet Katie one day, and she has the same woman's heart. Weirder yet, Bowie is married to Katie, and he used to be engaged to the woman who died and had her organs donated."

His eyes grew big, and so did hers because as soon as she turned into the gravel driveway, she saw the government vehicle with the large Department of Social Services emblem on the side.

She killed the engine and sat for a moment staring at

the car. "What are they doing here so soon?" She didn't mean to say it out loud.

"Are they here to take me away?" Will's voice grew high-pitched and frantic.

"No, they just want to make sure you're okay." She had hoped to have a few weeks or even months until they showed up for a welfare check.

An older woman with glasses and a head full of gray pin curls stepped from the sedan. She smoothed the wrinkles from her black pants and reached back inside for her clipboard.

Natalie took a big breath. "Let's go, Will."

He shook his head. "No. Let's leave."

"You're made from tougher stuff. Let's face her and get this over with." She opened her door and walked toward the woman. When Will continued to sit in the car, she waved at him to join her.

"Are you Natalie Keane?"

"Yes." Natalie leaned in to see the tiny letters of her nametag. *Fran Dougherty.* Below her name was her title, *Social Worker.* "I wasn't expecting you so soon."

Will left the car and moved to Natalie's side.

"We like to make our first visit unannounced. It's better to check in right away because the first few days are the hardest." She turned to Will. "How are you, Will?"

Green eyes watched her in a hard stare. "How do you think I am?"

She seemed to ponder his response. "I'm sure you're confused. You've had lots of changes in your life recently."

Natalie could see his fists forming and his body growing stiff. She laid her arm over his shoulders and pulled him to her side.

"Mrs. Dougherty just wants to make sure you're being taken care of. Shall we show her around?" She hoped her voice held more confidence than she felt.

Will looked up at her with an expression that begged for her not to let them take him.

"I won't," she whispered, hoping he knew what she meant.

"You seem familiar with the process," Fran said.

"Yes." Natalie walked them to the front door. "I grew up in the foster care system. My mother died when I was six."

Fran scribbled something on her paper and waited for Natalie to unlock the door.

"Do you have neighbors?" Fran asked, looking around. The only thing visible was the highway and the forest.

"Not really. The closest neighbors I have would be Abby Garrett and Cade Mosier. She owns a bee ranch, and he raises cattle."

"People ranch bees?" Will asked in awe. His once tense demeanor melted into excitement over the talk of insects.

"I don't know the right term for it, but she has a bunch of hives."

"I believe they are known as apiculturists," Fran added.

"Cool." Will stepped aside so Natalie could open the door.

They entered the home that once felt like a hug. Now it was cramped with the three of them jockeying for personal space.

"This is where you both live?" Fran quickly wrote notes across the page. "Where does Will sleep?"

They pointed to the loft.

"Where do you sleep, Natalie?"

She nodded toward the couch. She was grateful she'd tidied up this morning. Leaving a blanket on the couch made it appear like she hadn't cleaned all week. "I know it's small, but it provides us with all we need."

"Twelve-year-old boys need privacy. They also need friends. Have you registered him for school?"

Natalie shook her head. "He's been here for less than a week. And it's the beginning of summer. I'll put that on my list."

"Yes, it is summer, which means lots of idle hours. What's your plan for Will when you're at work?" She continued to make notes.

"He comes with me to the diner. He has his own table where he can draw and read."

"I'm not sure that's a healthy scenario. His body needs to move."

Natalie rubbed her forehead hard enough to make her skull ache. "I'll look into other arrangements."

"He'll also need a physical and immunizations, school supplies, and clothes."

Natalie listened to the extensive list of Will's needs and wanted to shout, *I QUIT!* When she looked at him and saw the excitement in his expression as he pointed to his new T-shirt, she stayed quiet.

"I got this today. I also went to the library and got a book."

Fran sighed. "I know you want to stay here, and I know your sister is trying to do what she thinks is right, but we're working with an odd situation." She smiled at Will. "It might be better if you went outside to play."

"Where? In the woods?" he asked.

Fran looked at Natalie with a see-what-I-mean look.

"Anything concerning Will should include Will." It wasn't fair that adults made all the decisions. "This situation affects Will, and he should have a say so."

"Fine," Fran huffed. "It might not be pleasant."

"You want to stay, Will?" Natalie asked.

His head bobbed. "Yes."

Natalie wanted to tell Fran that Will was used to unpleasant moments. Finding his father foamy mouthed and unresponsive wasn't something a kid should experience. Whatever she had to say was gravy.

Fran cleared her throat. "Why would a father leave custody of his son to a daughter he abandoned years ago? I have to wonder what he was thinking." Her expression turned grim. "Given his habits, there is the question of whether he was in his right mind or thinking at all."

Natalie had grown up fighting for everything. She didn't have much, but what she had was important. A week ago, she'd had no idea that Will was her brother, and now that she knew, she wouldn't let the Department of Social Services take him away.

"I understand this isn't your typical situation. It's obvious that I'm not set up for life with a teenage boy."

"It's more than that," Fran said.

"I know. Listen, I might be a total failure when it comes to raising him, but I want to try. People like Will and I have little. We weren't given a lot in the beginning. Take me away from him and he has even less, and vice versa. If you take him from me, you'll only put him with another stranger. They may have a better house. Maybe they'll have more resources, but they can't offer what I can, and that's the experience of knowing exactly what he's going through."

Fran looked around the tiny house and frowned. "This place is small and isolated. It's barely adequate for an adult."

A fire burned in Natalie's chest. She had felt nothing like it since she moved out of her final foster home, ready to prove to the world she had value. "What if I move to a bigger place?"

"That only solves one issue. He needs friends and peers. Teenagers are tough to raise. Even the most well-seasoned parents struggle."

"Give us a chance to prove you wrong." She looked at Will. "Get something to write on and something to write with. Let's make a list of things we need to do to satisfy Mrs. Dougherty's concerns."

Will pulled a pad of paper and a crayon from his backpack. "I'm ready."

Natalie stared at the green-eyed little boy who was proving to have as big a heart as he did an attitude.

They spent the next ten minutes making lists of things Fran would like to see from accommodations to healthy food. Natalie scoffed at that because peanut butter was a protein, and corn chips had to count as a vegetable.

"You've got a month to figure it out, or we'll have to look into a better setting for Will. There are lots of families who could offer him everything."

"No, they can't. I'm his sister. Show me a family who can top that." The steel around her heart fractured, and a flood of emotion overwhelmed her.

Fran left, and Natalie collapsed on the couch next to Will, who stared at the list.

"How do we pay for all this?" His voice warbled with emotion.

She inhaled deeply, pushing down her own desperate need to cry. "We beg, borrow, or steal. We'll make it happen, whatever it takes."

He swiped an errant tear from his cheek. "Don't forget rule number two—no stealing."

# CHAPTER EIGHT

Jake loved a good challenge, but he hadn't come to Aspen Cove to take on a new project. He was there to open B's Book Nook and get back home to negotiate the partnership he'd chased for years. Now that he was here, he couldn't help himself.

Each time he saw Will, he saw a boy with lots of potential but little opportunity. Then there was his sister, who pulled at him in different ways. She was tough yet vulnerable, closed off, but somehow still open. She was brave and still scared. He saw these things in her eyes. She hadn't told him her story, but those green eyes spoke of a lifetime of challenges.

He walked into Maisey's. It was summer, and the town grew busier each day. The booths and tables were filled with locals, tourists, and construction crews. The scent of bacon and maple syrup filled the air. In the corner booth was Will, who stared at his pancakes with a look of boredom etched across his face.

"Can I join you? I hate eating alone."

Will snapped his head up. "Sure. I'm used to eating alone, but I like company."

Jake took the napkin from the table and placed it on his lap. "Not a big appetite? Only pancakes today?"

He shrugged. "Not a big budget. I eat my sister's employee meal, and she doesn't want to take advantage."

Jake sat back and considered Will's statement. He knew they struggled financially. It was why Will had stolen the Harry Potter book. Limited money meant limited resources. If his memory served him right, when he was twelve, he could empty a refrigerator in two days.

Jake pulled the menu from the holder and set in on the table between them.

"If you could have anything on this menu, what would it be?"

Will's eyes grew wide. He turned the menu around so he could read it. Taking his time, he went through everything available.

"I like the pancakes, but I also like sausage."

"You didn't have sausage with yours today?"

His shoulders lifted with a breath and then sagged. "I did, but I ate them first, and now all I have left is the pancakes."

"But you'd eat more sausages if you had them?"

He rolled his eyes like Jake's question was idiotic.

Will was a growing boy. He'd probably eat anything that wasn't breathing and wouldn't kill him.

"You like bacon?"

"I do, but I like sausages better."

Natalie swung by. "Do you want tea or juice?"

Jake considered her question for a moment. "Let's live on the edge. I'll have juice and a chocolate milk."

She smirked at him. "Weird combination."

65

"Hey, don't knock what you haven't tried." He closed the menu and put it back in the holder. "Since I'm going wild, and swinging by the rafters, I thought maybe I'd have bacon and eggs and a double order of sausage." He looked at Will and winked.

"You accuse me of trying to kill you, and now you're killing yourself?" She shook her head.

"Life isn't worth living unless you take a few risks. Are you a risk-taker, Natalie?"

She nodded toward Will. "I must be because I took him." She left before he could reply.

"Are you trying to kill yourself?" Will picked up his fork, preparing to take a bite of pancake.

"Nah, I'm sharing my resources. The chocolate milk and sausages are for you. I can't have you starving if I plan to put you to work, can I?"

Will dropped the fork, and the clatter it made drew the attention of the surrounding tables who gave them a passing glance before returning to their conversations.

"You want me to work with you again today?"

"Do you want to come to the shop?"

He chewed his bottom lip and nodded. "I do, but I'm not sure Natalie will be okay with it. She doesn't want me to be a pest."

"How about you be my partner for the day?"

Natalie swung by to drop off the juice and chocolate milk. She eyed him before she handed the milk to Will. "Don't spoil him. I can't afford for him to get used to a life I can't sustain."

Will laughed. "You can't fool my sister."

"I can see that." He was about to ask if Will could come to the shop, but the door opened, and she shot toward the new customer like an arrow seeking a target.

Will drank deeply and came away with a milk mustache. He cocked his head in thought. "Can I ask you a question? I mean, since you're a life coach and all."

"Sure. I'll do my best to answer."

Will's lips drew into a thin line. "I heard somewhere that boys turn out to be exactly like their fathers." He chewed on his bottom lip. "Does that mean I will use drugs?"

It was an innocent question that punched Jake in the gut. Statistically, the odds were not in Will's favor. Children of drug addicts were twice as likely to be users themselves. That wasn't something he'd tell Will. Kids his age were sponges and soaked up information. He didn't want to plant a seed that might become a reality through suggestion.

"Absolutely not. You get to choose who you are. Everything we do in life is a choice. Each choice has a consequence. If I ate sausage and bacon and drank loads of soda, I'm deciding to compromise my new kidney. I used to eat and drink lots of those things. That was before I came down with kidney disease. I know those foods are bad for me, so I make a choice to avoid them." He emphasized the word *me* so Will would know it wasn't a blanket statement that applied to everyone.

"Right. Like I stole something, but I know better, and can make better choices."

"Exactly." He high-fived Will just as Natalie brought over the food.

"I'm assuming the sausages aren't for you either."

"You're smart ... and pretty."

Will laughed. "This time, you are totally hitting on my sister."

Jake shook his head. "There's no crime in complimenting a beautiful woman." He looked up at her and watched her lips lift into a smile, but as fast as the smile came, it left, and she was off running again.

"Your sister seems stressed. Are you guys, okay?"

Will shoved a sausage into his mouth and spoke around it. "Not really. Lots of shi—stuff going on."

"Anything I can help with?" He picked up his turkey bacon and took a bite. He made a point of chewing with his mouth closed so Will would get the idea. When he swallowed, he spoke again. "If you need something, it's better to ask than do without."

He shrugged. "It's okay. People like us are used to doing without."

Another punch rocked his insides. "People like you?" He was afraid to ask what Will meant, but he needed to know. "What's that mean?"

He leaned in and whispered. "The people no one cares about. The ones no one wants."

A boulder-sized lump lodged in Jake's throat. He chewed another piece of bacon while he pondered how to answer. This was the kind of stuff that fell in his lane, but none of his clients had ever been preteen boys who felt worthless. He glanced toward Natalie, who leaned against the counter and stared back. Did she feel the same? Was she exactly the woman Maisey described? Was she afraid of jumping in with both feet because it was too risky?

"Just because you feel unloved at the moment doesn't mean you are unloved." He chanced another look at Natalie, who continued to stare at him. What did she see when her eyes narrowed in his direction? They seemed to ask if he was a friend or foe. "Your sister cares for you. If she didn't, she wouldn't give you her meal."

Will forked a bite of pancake and was about to shove it in his mouth when he stopped and put it down. "It's not that. If she doesn't feed me, Social Services will take me away."

He said it matter of fact like he was talking about the weather.

"I'm sorry about your father, Will."

His lip quivered. "Do you think my father ever loved me, or did he love the drugs more?"

Jake inhaled and let out the breath in a whoosh. "I'm sure he loved you, but he made bad choices, and that's a lesson you can learn. It might be the greatest lesson your father ever taught you. When you make poor decisions, it affects everyone."

He nodded and went back to eating his pancakes.

Natalie walked over with the bill. "If you don't need anything else, I'll leave this here. No rush."

He reached out for her hand before she could run away. A single touch sent a jolt through him. She seemed to be the only woman who affected him that way. It was either that or static electricity in the air. He stopped a moment to gather his wits. "Can Will come back to the shop and help again today?"

She stared down at where his hand touched hers. Was she feeling the same heat he did? Was it possible to feel connected to someone he didn't know?

She pulled free and turned to Will, who sat straight and looked at her with a hopeful expression. "Do you want to go to the bookstore?"

He loved the way she involved him. By asking, she made him feel included and responsible for his decisions, which would only help him make better choices in the future.

"I do."

Each time she looked at Will, her eyes softened. "Okay. Don't be a pest, and if he says he's had enough of you, come back to the diner."

"He'll be fine. We've got books to order, and if I'm lucky, applications to sift through." He considered their situation. "Hey, what about you? Are you interested in working at the Book Nook?"

She frowned and shook her head. "I waitress. That's what I know. That's what I do."

Will piped in, "Yeah, but you could make a different choice."

She turned around and walked away.

Jake put enough money on the table to cover their breakfasts and a hefty tip. "Grab your things and come on. We've got books that need readers."

When he arrived at the Book Nook, Mrs. Brown and Bailey were standing at the door. "Back for another go?"

"I'm a glutton for punishment," she said.

He opened the door and turned to Will. "Why don't you take Bailey to the kid's books and help her pick out something she'll like? Make sure she doesn't get into anything else." He leaned in and quickly told Will the details. Surprise colored Will's face, but he offered Bailey his hand and led her to the children's books where he pulled out a few until she picked *The Very Hungry Caterpillar*. They slid to the floor, and Will started to read, using different voices for different characters.

"Your son is amazing with her. Maybe you should start a story hour."

Jake didn't correct her. Will wasn't his son, but if he had one, he'd be proud for him to be like Will. He wasn't a bad kid; he'd just had a bad life. Will would grow up to be a fine man if given love, support, and boundaries.

———

JUST AFTER TWO O'CLOCK, Natalie walked in, looking worn and worried. She glanced around and leaned on the counter.

"Hey, Jake," she said with no inflection to her voice. "Where's Will?"

He was certain if she wasn't holding on to the wood countertop, she'd be in a heap on the floor. "He's in the office looking at porn," he teased.

"Okay," she said on an exhale.

He counted to himself and got to three when her head snapped up, and her jaw fell open. "He's what?"

Jake laughed. "You have life left in you after all. When you entered, I thought you were a zombie."

"I feel like one. Who knew having a kid around would be so exhausting?"

He walked around the corner and put his hand on her back, then led her to a table. She collapsed onto the chair.

"I'm sure it's challenging, but what's got you so beat?" It was a good choice of words because she looked not only tired but ready to give up.

She rubbed at her eyes. With her elbows on the table, she cradled her head and sighed. "Nothing I can't handle."

When she looked at him, doubt turned her once clear eyes cloudy with concern.

"I'm sure you can handle it. Something tells me you can handle more than the average person, but that doesn't mean you have to do it alone."

"That's the only way I know." She grabbed the edge of the table and attempted to stand, but he placed his hand on top of her arm.

"Stay with me and talk for a few minutes." He glanced toward the door at the back of the store. "Will is fine. He's in the office looking at pictures of reading nooks and picking out stuff for a kid's corner. Someone suggested a great idea."

"I'm not running your register." She leaned back and crossed her arms.

He took in her body language. This was a perfect example of nature versus nurture. Her and Will's mannerisms were identical.

"Okay, but what if Will did a story hour each week? We can call it Winding Down with Will."

Was that a tear he saw in the corner of her eye? She swiped at it. "He loves to read, but ..." She swallowed hard. "I'm ... I'm not sure—" She covered her face and let out a squeak.

"Come here." He could see she was ready to crack and took her hand to lead her around the corner where no one could see her cry. He stopped in front of the romance section and stood before her. He lifted her chin, really getting the first close look at her where she wasn't rushing away from him.

God, she was pretty. Silky brown hair, alabaster skin, and those eyes filled with tears that only made them glow a brighter green. "What's wrong?" His hands slipped to her shoulders to keep her there. He watched as silent tears spilled down her cheeks.

She shook her head, and the more she tried to control her emotions, the more she trembled. He hated to watch people crumble. Hated that she didn't feel like she had anyone to share her problems with.

"Hey." He cupped her cheek and thumbed the tears away. "I'm here. I'll listen. Tell me what's wrong." His hand slid around her back to pull her closer. He expected her to fight the affection or to bolt, but she didn't. She sank against him and sobbed. He held her for minutes while she emptied her sorrows against his chest. His hands brushed up and down her back while his lips skimmed the top of her head between whispers of affirmation and offers of help.

"What do you need?"

She jumped back. "I need to go."

He moved forward and cupped her cheek. It would have been so easy to kiss her, but he didn't. "I'm here when you need me."

She laughed, but it wasn't one of happiness. "Everyone says that, but they don't mean it."

"I mean it."

"Jake?" Will called from the office. "What about bean bag chairs?"

He stepped away. "My designer has a question. Stay here; I'll be right back."

He walked to the office to look at what had excited Will and found he'd picked out several brightly colored bean bags. "These are washable, so that's good, right?"

"Those could work."

Natalie appeared at the door. She hid the proof of her tears with sunglasses. "Hey, bud, it's time to go. We've got that list to take care of."

Will jumped up and high-fived Jake as he passed. "Are we going to get the bean bags?"

"Maybe. Let's plan a trip to Copper Creek and see

what they have too." He turned to look at Natalie. "Care to join us?"

"I'm always working, but if Will wants to join you, I'm okay with that."

He nodded, not ready to press her harder for fear she'd walk away.

"Are you going home?"

"We've got some things to do, and then yes, we're headed home."

Will laughed. "It's not really a home. Harry Potter had it better living under the stairs."

"Not funny," she said.

Jake laughed on the way to the door. "But is it true?"

# CHAPTER NINE

"Are you kidding me?" She looked at Mason Van der Veen with disbelief. "There's a hole in the middle of the floor." She leaned over and watched a mouse scurry across the dirt into the darkened corner.

"It's the only house I have that's not on the docket for refurbishing this year." He started for the door. "You said you were desperate."

"For a new place. Not a broken leg or hantavirus."

"Can't help you then." He waited for her to step outside. When she did, he turned to lock the door.

She couldn't figure out why he felt the need. There was nothing to steal. The avocado-colored countertops hadn't seen use since the seventies. Half the lights were missing. When she turned on the water, it came out looking like pumpkin puree.

"This is what I've got for what you're willing to pay."

"Nope, this won't work." She rushed to her car before she had a meltdown in front of a complete stranger.

It had been a week since the social worker's visit. Each day, she fit in time to look at a rental. Anything affordable was outside of town, which didn't fit Will's need for socialization. This one seemed promising until she drove up and saw the sagging porch and broken windows. Even that didn't dissuade her. She could figure out how to get new panes. Maybe even ask Baxter or Wes if they could shore up the porch. She'd find a way to make payments, but the hole in the living room floor was too much.

She leaned her head against the steering wheel and took deep breaths hoping they'd slow down the thundering of her heart. When it continued to flutter, she turned the key and listened to her Subaru choke and spit before the engine caught and lurched forward.

She got one block before the check engine light glowed red like a demon's eye, and the car lost power and rolled to a stop by the curb.

"Not now!" she screamed and beat the steering wheel with her palms.

Her chest hurt, and her lungs seized. She struggled to take a breath and felt everything tighten as if a fist were twisting her organs. Certain she was nearing death, she opened the car door and fell out. The asphalt cut into her knees, but it was nothing compared to the pain in her chest. She scrambled to her feet and took off. It was a half run, half stumble until she fell through the pharmacy door and collapsed on the entry floor.

Agatha lifted up from her chair to see her. "Doc," she yelled. "We've got a live one."

She moved around the counter to kneel beside Natalie, who held her chest and sucked in gulps of air. "I'm dying."

"Who's dying?" Doc asked as he lumbered toward her, wearing his bright orange Crocs. When he saw

Natalie on the floor, he turned and yelled. "Lydia, I need your help."

Natalie wasn't sure what would kill her first, the embarrassment or the pain.

Dr. Lydia ran to the front, followed by her sister Sage who was the nurse for the clinic. They took in the scene in front of them.

"I'll get the gurney," Sage said and turned to leave.

"No, help me up." Natalie raised a hand. "I can make it."

Doc glanced down his crooked nose. "Then why are you cleaning my floor with your clothes?"

She breathed in choppy breaths and let out a wail that would make a dog howl. "I'm sorry. I don't ..." She attempted to stand, but her will to push forward was gone, and she fell to the floor again.

"Here you go." Lydia helped lift her from one side while Sage got the other. Between the two women, they managed to get her to the exam room.

She looked around and found Peter Larkin sitting on the chair in the corner.

"You read that karmer suter too?"

Doc handed him a tube of Bengay and a bottle of ibuprofen. He pointed to the door. "It's Kama Sutra. Now, go home, Peter, and stop twisting yourself into knots. You're eighty, not eighteen."

He pointed at Natalie. "Maybe, but at least I walked in here by myself."

Natalie climbed onto the table and curled into a ball on her side. Lydia checked her pupils while Sage measured her blood pressure. She was convinced she'd had a heart attack and was nearing a stroke.

As soon as Peter left, Doc took his seat. "You want to tell me what brought on this attack?"

Through sobs, she said, "Too much fried food?"

"Not likely at your age." He pulled the chair forward, so they were face to face while Lydia put away supplies, and Sage walked out the door.

"Talk to me, Natalie."

"Am I having a heart attack?"

Lydia stood at the head of the exam table. "No, you're having a panic attack."

Sage walked inside the room, holding a bottle of water.

"That's it? I came here thinking I was dying, and it's just a panic attack? How am I supposed to pay you, fix my car, and find an appropriate place to live?"

"Let's figure it out," Doc answered. "What's got you spun up?"

He opened a floodgate with his question. Normally she would have said nothing and walked away, but she knew if she rolled off the exam table, she'd hit the floor and never rise again. Will needed her, and she was failing him.

"I don't know where to start." She curled into a tighter ball.

Sage offered her the water. "Sit up, and let's take it from the beginning."

She rolled to her bottom and took in a shaky breath. After a drink of water, she lifted the floodgates and let her problems spill out.

"This was a mistake. I can't afford to be here," she started. "Will should be the one sitting on the exam table. He needs a school physical and shots." She opened her mouth to continue.

Doc raised his hand. "No bill. We have it covered."

"Why would you do that?"

A grumble filled the air. "Because we're a community, which is just another word for family."

She set the water bottle down and rubbed her face with her palms. "I bit off more than I can chew."

"Take smaller bites," Lydia said.

Doc cleared his throat. "Dr. Lydia is right. When you get a piece of pie, you don't eat it all at once."

Natalie dropped her hands and lowered her head. "You haven't seen me eat pie."

"Okay, problem number one is taken care of," Doc said. "You're not dying, and Will will get what he needs. Move on."

"My car broke down. I was looking for a house. The social worker will take my brother away if I can't get a new place where he has his own room." Her throat closed, and a squeak escaped. "I can't find a place if I don't have a car." Her heart started to race again. Talking about the problems didn't help. It only pointed out the magnitude of insurmountable issues she faced.

Doc pulled his phone from his pocket. He punched in a few numbers and waited.

"Bobby, I need you to tow a car to the garage and figure out what's wrong with it."

Everyone was silent except Doc, who shook his head. "Not my car. It's Natalie's car." He cupped the receiver and asked, "Where's it at?"

She shook her head. "Haven't you heard a word I said? I can't afford to fix it." Tears ran down her cheeks.

"I didn't ask you how you'd pay for it. I asked where it was."

"It's on Daisy Lane."

He relayed the information, hung up, and asked Sage to get the keys and meet Bobby outside.

Natalie looked at the clock on the wall, and the panic set in again. "Oh my God, I'm late getting back for my shift."

Doc called Agatha to the room and asked her to tell Maisey that Natalie wouldn't be back in for the day, and that it might be better to get Louise to fill in a few of her shifts.

"No, I need the money." She was certain the old doctor was deaf or suffering from dementia.

Doc took her hand and held it in the same manner Jake had. "Everything will work out."

It was a caring gesture and nicked at her heart. She'd been in town for over a year and had invested no time in getting to know the people. She knew their names and what they did, but outside of the superficial, she was at a loss. Her head swam with a hundred reasons, none of which made her neglect okay.

She nearly choked. Was she like her father? What was the difference between abandoning people and living in the same town but ignoring them? Her lack of humanity had to be a family trait.

Even Jake had tried to get to know her. He'd tried to comfort her, and she ran because the sexy man was like a peanut butter cup. Once she got a taste of him, his kindness, and his care, she'd want more.

"Okay," Lydia said. "Will should be fine, and your car will be fixed. What's next?"

She could have told them she'd handle it all, but obviously, she couldn't.

"The housing situation. I live in a tiny house between here and Copper Creek. It's like living in a matchbox. It worked when I was alone, but it won't long-term. I've been searching for an affordable rental." She let her head hang. "I don't make enough money at the diner to afford much. Business is picking up, but ..."

Lydia raised her hand. "Let me see what I can do. I'm married to a home builder. He might have an idea."

All the stress of the last week slipped from her body. She could have easily rolled to her side and slept for a week, but that wasn't an option. Will was at the bookstore with Jake again, and she needed to pick him up and feed him.

"I've got to go. Will is probably driving Jake crazy."

Doc lifted from his chair. "Something tells me that Jake can handle a lot. Looks to me like that boy already has."

It struck her funny that Doc referred to Jake as a boy. When she looked at him, all she saw was a hot, virile man. If she closed her eyes, she could almost relive the moment when he held her. Being in his arms caused her to want things she had no business wanting.

Since that day, he hadn't touched her, but the fire she saw in his eyes each time he looked at her said he wanted to.

"How do I repay you for all of this?"

Doc wrinkled his brow. "Next time I'm at the diner, I get a bigger piece of pie."

Natalie laughed. "I can do that."

Lydia helped her down. On her way out of the exam room, she told her to try to relax and handed her a printout with breathing exercises. "I'll get back to you about your living situation as soon as I talk to Wes. He's in Cross Creek helping the Lockhart brothers with a project." At the door, she stopped and pulled Natalie in for a hug. In the last week, she'd experienced more affection than she had in years—maybe a lifetime.

She started toward B's Book Nook to get Will so they could go home when she realized she had no way to get there.

# CHAPTER TEN

"Excuse me, what did you say?" Jake's heart rate picked up as he waited for Matt Steinman, the president of Vision Quest, to continue.

"Listen, Jake, I know this was not part of the plan, but another candidate presented himself, and it would be irresponsible for us to not interview him. This is a big undertaking—a huge change. Maybe your delay in signing on was actually a blessing."

The door opened, and Natalie walked in. She looked as down and depressed as he felt. He covered the phone with his hand. "Will is almost finished with his story hour." She nodded and took a seat at a nearby table.

"What does this mean for me?" he asked Matt.

"It means a few more weeks of uncertainty. I hate to do that to you, but we have to pick the best man for the job."

"Who's my competition?"

"Fritz Laughlin," Matt answered.

Jake let out a heavy sigh. It was a small world at this level of coaching, but Fritz was a solid candidate. Head-to-head, they probably looked evenly matched, but Jake knew he'd come out the victor because Fritz, while good at his job, thrived on notoriety. That was probably his interest in the position. That was part of the allure to Jake too, but only part. Partnering with Vision Quest would make him a household name, but the work was just as important to him.

"You do what you have to."

They said goodbye, and he hung up and walked around the corner to where Natalie sat at the table near the door.

"Hey, how are you?"

She pulled herself up to sit taller. "I'm okay."

He hadn't seen her much since that day in the stacks where she'd cried, and he had offered comfort. Outside of his breakfast visits in the diner and her picking up Will, he had had little time with her, and yet, somehow, he missed her. Missed her wit, and also her intelligence. She was smart and well-read.

"You look like you could use another hug." He pulled out the chair and sat beside her.

"By the sounds of your conversation, it seems like you need a hug too."

He chuckled and smiled. "Are you offering?"

She shouldered him but stayed leaning against his side. "I'm not much of a nurturer."

He wrapped his arm around her and pulled her closer. "That's probably not true, but I imagine you haven't seen nurturing in action."

"Understatement." She sighed and laid her head against his shoulder while they listened to Will read a *Pete the Cat* book.

Will looked up and saw his sister leaning against Jake, and a grin spread across his face.

"Next time I'm reading *Green Eggs and Ham* by Dr. Seuss," Will told the kids. All of Louise's kids were present, as was Bowie and Katie's daughter Sahara, and Bailey Brown, who sat in the front so Will could make sure nothing ended up inside her nose. "See you next time."

Louise, Katie, and Mallory appeared from the aisles and swept up their kids. As they walked out, Agatha walked in.

She stood before him and Natalie. "Are you giving her and Will a ride back home?" She shook her keys in the air. "Doc sent me over to do the job, but if you got it under control, I'd rather go home and kick up my feet." She touched her forehead with the back of her hand. "That one gave us a scare today."

Natalie sat up and moved away. "No, I'll call a cab. Will and I are fine."

Agatha waved her hand through the air. "You are not fine. If you were, you wouldn't have crumbled on the floor of the pharmacy."

He twisted his body to look at her. "What happened?" He laid his hand on her shoulder, but she shrugged him off and glanced at Will, who was straightening up the books by the reading nook.

"It was nothing."

Knowing Natalie wouldn't share anything else, he looked at Agatha. "Was it nothing?"

She stared at Natalie as if debating how much to tell him. "You know, young lady, it's okay to ask for help. It doesn't mean you're weak or incapable. All it means is you need help, and right now, you need a ride." She turned back to Jake. "Surely you can close early and help her out."

He was happy to help. "You bet."

Agatha gave them a final glance before walking to the door. "You two look great together."

"We're not ..." When the door closed behind them, Natalie turned to him. "Seriously, I can figure it out."

He rose from the chair and walked to the entrance, turning the open sign to closed.

"You could. Of that, I'm sure, but you don't have to." He nodded to Will, who was coming back from the office with his backpack slung over his shoulder. Two weeks ago, he would have wanted to look inside to make sure the boy hadn't stolen anything, but now he wasn't worried. He'd built a relationship with Will. One that he knew meant more to the kid than a book.

"But—"

"But nothing." He walked around the counter to get his keys and moved to the back door. "Hey, Will, remember that trip to Copper Creek?"

The kid's eyes lit up. "Yeah."

"Seems as if I have you and your sister as hostages for a bit. I thought maybe if you're game, and your sister doesn't complain too much, we can look for bean bags for the kid's nook. If you're hungry, I hear there's a great pizza place called Piper's."

Natalie shook her head. "Oh, we can't—"

"Pleeease," Will begged. "I haven't had pizza in a lifetime."

Natalie looked at her brother, and he could see her waiver.

Jake moved in front of her. "Pleeease," he mimicked Will.

"You two are impossible."

"So that's a yes?" Will asked.

Her lips pulled into a thin line. "I guess, but don't think begging works all the time."

Will leaped into the air with a "Woo hoo."

Jake opened the back door. Will walked out first and before Natalie could follow, Jake stopped her and pulled her in for a hug. "This one was for me, and if it helps you along the way, that's a bonus."

After the shock wore off, she tilted her head and smiled. "You're too much."

"Sweetheart, I'm just enough." He got everyone in the SUV, and before he started the engine, he said, "What's first? Food or shopping?"

The unanimous decision was to forage for food first, so they'd have the energy to shop.

"Nice car," Will said from the back seat.

"It's a rental."

"Still nice," Natalie added. She leaned forward and brushed her fingers across the wood inlay on the dash. "Acura?"

"RDX," he answered. "I heard the weather was unpredictable, and I didn't want to get caught unprepared."

"Good thinking. I have an old Subaru. When it's working, it's great, but today not so much."

"What's wrong with it?"

She let out a long exhale. "No idea. I was looking at a potential rental property, and on the way back, it spit and sputtered and then died."

He felt awful for her. That was the way of the world it seemed. Life always kicked a person when they were down. It had him. He'd gotten the news that his kidneys were failing, and a week later, his fiancée Jenny had left him. She couldn't handle the implications of being with a man who had a life-threatening disease.

"Where is it now?"

"Doc had Louise's husband, Bobby, tow it to his shop." She twisted her hands together in her lap. "Doc saw me for free and said he'd be happy to do Will's school physical. Bobby is fixing my car. I hate owing anyone, and now I owe so many people." A little growl escaped before she could stop it.

He reached over and took her hand. "You don't owe anything. Sometimes people do things because it makes them feel good. Don't take that away from them."

He kept his hand wrapped around hers until they reached Piper's Pizza.

Will jumped out as soon as they came to a stop. Jake turned to Natalie.

"Bringing you two to dinner makes me feel good. Just go with it. Besides, Will works hard when he's at the bookstore. He deserves a night out. Let the stress of the day go and enjoy the moment."

He got out and raced around to open her door. When they walked inside the restaurant, Will was already seated in a booth, looking over the menu.

"Will?" He raised a brow. "You and I will have to chat about manners." He glanced at Natalie to make sure he wasn't overstepping his boundaries. He moved aside so she could slide into the booth, and he sat beside her. "You should have opened the door for your sister and walked her inside."

Will frowned. "She's not my date."

"She doesn't have to be. It's a common courtesy. When you grow up, you'll want people to respect you, but respect is earned through small actions every day. Watch how a person behaves in their personal life, and you'll know how they are professionally."

He let his head hang, and his shoulders slump. "I'm only twelve."

"And a role model to so many kids in town. Look at how they look up to you at the bookstore. You're like a rock star." He watched as Will grew taller with each compliment. "Being a role model comes with responsibilities. Are you up to the task?"

Will seemed to ponder his options. "As long as I don't have to pick Bailey's nose, I'm in."

Natalie laughed. "I've heard about her."

Jake chuckled. "Her mother says she's a Houdini with beans."

The waitress arrived to take their order. They ordered one meat lovers and one vegetarian. He rarely indulged in pizza because the salt content was so high, but today he'd follow his own advice. He'd let it all go and enjoy the time he had with Will and Natalie.

Will pointed to the game room. "Can I have money to play pinball?"

Natalie dug through her purse for quarters, but Jake gave Will a five and told him to be back in fifteen minutes.

"You're spoiling him," she said after he dashed away.

"I'm indulging him. I'm not spoiling him. There's a difference. I don't think Will is the spoilable type."

"I suppose you're right. He's had so little in his life."

The waitress dropped off Will's root beer and Jake's and Natalie's waters.

"I get the impression that you haven't had much more."

"Oh, I do okay. When I was his age, it was the same. If

89

it hadn't been for free lunch at school, I would have had one meal a day."

"That's why he's so important to you." It wasn't a question but a statement. "You say you're not a nurturer, but you took in a kid you didn't know, and you're doing everything you can to make sure he's better off than you were. I'd say that's supportive."

A blush flooded her cheeks with color. "I'm trying, but I'm failing."

"Do you want to talk about it?"

"Have you got a week?"

"I do. Turns out, my plans have changed a bit. I was desperate to be out of town as soon as possible, but I've hit a snag."

She turned, and her knee brushed against his thigh.

"Would *you* like to talk about it?" she asked.

Natalie was great at deflecting. He was certain it was a learned trait.

"After you. Tell me about Social Services."

She moved her head around.

He could hear her neck pop into place.

"You'll see when you drop us off on the way back. We live halfway in between here and Aspen Cove."

"Really? Me too." He lifted his shoulders. "I don't live here, but I'm staying in a one-room cabin next to Tilden Cool's house."

She cocked her head. "Oh, then we're neighbors." She pulled a pen from her purse and drew on her napkin. "If you take the first right instead of going straight on Country Road 5, you'll find me. I'm that tiny trailer-like house on the right."

"I pass that every morning." He slapped the table.

"This is perfect. I can pick you up and take you home every day while your car is in the shop."

She shook her head. "Oh no, you don't have to."

He set his hand on top of hers. He did that a lot. He liked the way his palm covered it, the way the heat somehow traveled from her body into his. There was definitely a connection between them. Each touch sent a thread of heat weaving through his body. This one landed in his heart.

"I want to. Don't take that away from me. Helping you gives me purpose and value."

"You're a life coach. You have value and purpose already."

"By whose measurement?"

The pizza arrived, and Natalie stretched her neck to see if Will was coming. "Should I get him?"

"Let's wait."

"But the pizza will get cold."

"Not for us. If he's not back, then that's a consequence for him."

They started eating. Will returned fifteen minutes later.

"Ah, the cheese isn't melty anymore."

Jake looked at Natalie to see if she would address the situation. She nodded.

"Will, Jake asked you to be back in fifteen minutes. It's been thirty. If you would have come back when he said, then your pizza would have been hot and melty."

"But I was winning."

Jake understood. He'd been a kid once. "You made a choice. Now you have to live with the consequences."

Will narrowed his eyes and frowned. "Consequences suck but okay. Cold pizza is better than no pizza." After his first bite, the furrow between his brows smoothed. "Cold pizza isn't that bad either." He shoved in another bite and opened to talk around it.

Natalie reached over and chucked his chin. "Eat or talk, but don't do both at once."

Will swallowed. "Jeez, you'd think I was dining with the president."

Jake shook his head. "Wouldn't it be great if you could? Better yet, what if you had table manners that wouldn't make you question yourself if you were dining with him?"

The good thing about Will was that he wanted to do better.

"Do you think I'd ever have a chance to eat at the White House?"

"Sure, why not? You realize that the president was a twelve-year-old boy who probably ate with his mouth open once too. When you know better, you do better." Jake flagged down the waitress and asked for a box to take the leftovers home in. "How about you finish up, and we go to Costco and see what they have for the Winding Down with Will time at the bookstore?"

He smiled and was about to talk with his mouth full but held up a finger and swallowed. "I feel like Oprah. I have my own talk show." He laughed. "My audience isn't all that old, but hey, it's a start."

Jake reached over and ruffled Will's hair. "Everyone's got to start somewhere."

He paid the bill, and they headed toward the big-box store. Taking Will to Costco was like leading a starving man to a buffet. By the time they left, they had a flatbed of stuff like markers and paper for Saturday crafts, and a Lego table to occupy the kids while their parents shopped. Jake couldn't say no. He loved the light shining in the boy's eyes. Will was no longer thinking about what he could take, but what he could give.

They also piled the cart high with food, from fruits and veggies to bulk meats and grains. The only time he put a kibosh on anything Will suggested was when he asked for bowls of candy. Jake had to remind him that candy would have the opposite effect on what winding down set out to do.

Back in the SUV, Will chatted about all the things they could do on craft Saturdays. Things like make book-marks and book collages. He was so excited that as soon as the car stopped, he raced to the front door, talking about making samples. When he turned around, his eyes grew big, and he ran back and opened the door for his sister.

"Sorry, I forgot."

"They say it takes a month to create a habit." Natalie slid from the seat to the ground and turned around to look at Jake. "Thank you for everything."

Jake exited the car and walked around to open the back. "Hey, Will, come and help me."

Natalie rushed around to where he stood. "What are you doing?"

"You get half the food. Do you think I can eat all that by myself?"

"No. We can't take it."

Will picked up the case of Pop-Tarts. "Yes, we can." He took the keys from his sister's hand and ran to the door.

"Jake, it's too much."

"You're right, that's the problem with buying in bulk. It costs about half the price, but you have to buy so much of it. You'd be helping me out." He squatted down, so they were eye to eye. "Take it, Natalie. Don't say no."

She forced a smile to her face then nodded. "Thank you."

He helped unload items from the car and brought them into her home. It surprised him how small it was inside. If he stood sideways and stretched out his arms, he could almost touch both walls.

"I know it's not much, but when I was alone, it was perfect. Kind of like a hug." She unpacked items and used the zipper bags he'd bought to divide it up.

"It's small, but it fits you."

She kept the place tidy and homey looking. There were small touches around that made him smile. Little plaques that had affirmations like *Stay Strong,* and *Always Remember That You Are Braver Than You Think, and Stronger Than You Seem.* Those were often the things he said to his clients.

"It fits like a glove that's a size too small now. If I don't find a place soon"—she looked for Will, who was up in the loft cutting paper strips—"I might lose him." She swallowed hard. "Social Services gave us a list." She pointed to a page of notes written in purple crayon. The first line said, *New house.*

"That's quite a big list." He ran his finger down the items. Most were reasonable. On the bottom was a date circled several times.

"I'm running out of time." Her voice cracked.

"You've still got a few weeks."

She sniffled and nodded. "Yep. A few weeks." A tear ran down her cheek.

He looked up at Will, who was oblivious to anything

going on around him. "Hey," he said, wiping the tear away. "A lot can happen in three weeks."

He stared at her lips. They were rosy red and quivering. How much energy did it take to hold it all in?

"Sorry, I'm not usually so emotional."

"Nothing to be sorry about." He wanted to comfort her—needed to comfort her. "Help me take my half to the SUV?"

"You bet." She picked up the Ziplock bags and led the way. "Will," she called over her shoulder, "I'll be right back."

He lifted his head and lowered it to go back to work.

They tucked the groceries in the back and closed the hatch.

"Thank you for being such a great role model for him. He never stops talking about you."

"He's a smart kid."

She raised a brow. "Arrogant much?"

"Not what I meant."

She rocked back on her feet as if gaining momentum. On the third surge forward, she lifted onto her tiptoes and kissed his cheek.

Not willing to let that go by, he held her shoulders and leaned down to brush his lips against hers. He waited for her to shrug him off and move away, but she didn't.

Her arms slid up his back, and her head tilted while she moved in for another kiss. It was a gentle pass, an almost imperceptible touch, but he felt it on a deeper level. She was letting her guard down for a moment with him. Her hold grew tighter, and she leaned back to stare at him.

When her tongue slicked out to moisten her lips, he lost all sense of right or wrong. All he knew was that in the next second, her mouth would be his. One hand moved to her hip while the other cradled her head, holding her in place, waiting for her to say no.

He leaned forward and touched his mouth to hers, licking at the seam of her lips until she opened them. He wasted no time exploring the taste and texture of her. This wasn't the sweet and gentle kiss it had started out to be. This was more.

It was filled with desperation and loneliness, but he wasn't certain if it was his or hers. The vibrations of her moan made him want more, but clarity came crashing back, and he ended the kiss with a nip at her bottom lip and a step backward.

"That probably shouldn't have happened. I will only say I'm sorry for one reason, and that was because you were vulnerable, and I took advantage. But that kiss ... I'll never be sorry about that." He leaned against the SUV and watched for her reaction.

"I'm stronger than I seem."

"In that case—" He leaned in and kissed her again. Only this time, he switched their positions and pressed her between his body and the SUV. The pressure of his mouth on hers was all he craved. She was like a sweet liquor that he wanted to drink in. No, he needed to devour. She was the perfect mix of sweet, sexy, and vulnerable. It was a heady concoction for a man like him. A man who gave up love for work. He mentally shook that thought away. He hadn't given up on love; love had given up on him.

Kissing Natalie reminded him how much he needed this connection. How much he wanted to stay there and kiss her longer. How much the touch of a human being could change a life. At that thought, he broke the kiss.

His head shook, but his eyes focused on her mouth. "It's not right for me to kiss you like this, not when I know I'm leaving."

She slicked her tongue over her lips. "That's okay; you're my favorite kind of guy."

He quirked a brow. "What kind is that?"

"Temporary." She pressed a kiss to his lips and turned to walk away.

# CHAPTER ELEVEN

She'd kissed him. Or had he kissed her? She touched her lips, remembering yesterday's temporary lapse in judgment. Men like Jake were hazardous. They pulled her in with their kisses and kind words and left her wanting more. More was always dangerous.

As she waited outside with Will, she couldn't figure out why she'd agreed to have Jake pick them up. There was no pressing business in town. Doc had arranged for Louise to cover her shift, which meant she had nothing to do. The time was better spent looking for a place to live, but that required a car.

Her heart galloped inside her chest. What would Social Worker Fran say now? Things were worse than before. She had less money because of the loss of her shift. Her car wasn't working, and she still didn't have a suitable place for Will to live.

Feeling the panic set in, she took several deep breaths.

"When is he coming?" Will asked. He circled her like an excited puppy. In one hand was his backpack filled with bookmarks he'd made the night before. In his other hand was his fourth Harry Potter book. Jake had given it to him a few days before for his hard work.

"He'll get here when he gets here." Her eyes focused on the cloud of dust rolling down the road. "Looks like he's here." She pointed to the blue SUV turning into her long gravel driveway.

Jake came to a stop in front of them. He jumped out of the car and moved to Natalie's passenger side door.

"Are you going to nag at me for not opening it?" Will asked. "It's too early to think about manners."

"Manners, once learned, will become habit," Jake replied.

"Sheesh," Will said and climbed inside.

Jake held on to the handle for a moment without pulling the door open. He gazed at her eyes. "How are you today?"

How was it that a simple question, and the nearness of him, sent her entire body into chaos? Her heart raced. Her core pulsed. Her head grew dizzy.

"I'm okay."

He smiled, and her knees grew weak.

"Good to hear. I thought about you all night."

Her weak knees gave out.

Jake's hand left the handle and caught her before she hit the ground.

She looked down as if the gravel beneath her feet was the problem. "Rolled my ankle on a rock," she said, trying to cover up the truth: that his words, his voice, his touch, his kisses all had an effect on her.

"Right." He reached around, skimming his arm across hers, and pulled open the door. "Let's get you inside, so you don't find yourself in a puddle again."

Her jaw dropped. How did he know she was reduced

to a puddle when he was around? She'd done her best to pretend she was disinterested in Jake. *Liar, I kissed him like a love-starved idiot.*

She climbed inside and buckled up. When he rounded the SUV, she ignored him until he handed her a thermal cup.

"I made you chamomile tea."

She was done for. How was she supposed to remain indifferent to a man so thoughtful? "Thank you." Her fingers grazed his during the exchange. "What's on your agenda today?"

He glanced to the cargo section of the SUV. "Helping Will set up his reading corner, and then I've got some coaching calls to make. I'm hoping Agatha can help me out today. What about you?" He backed up and turned around to head toward town.

She sipped her tea and stared straight ahead. "I don't know. I've never had a day off where I didn't have something to do. I should be looking for a place to live, but with my car in the shop, that will be difficult." She turned around to look at Will. "If it weren't for him, I probably would have stayed home to read."

Jake turned from Country Road 5 on to the main highway. "Lucky for you, I own a bookstore."

"But it's not a library," Will piped in.

Jake chuckled. "Your sister can read what she wants."

"Hey," Will complained. "That's not fair. How come she gets different rules than me?"

"Because she doesn't dogear the books, and she's prettier."

Will laughed. "That's because you've never seen me in a dress."

They both chanced a look at him.

"Teasing," Will said and went back to his book.

They drove the rest of the way to town in relative silence with an occasional "No way" or "Cool" coming from the back seat.

"We're here," Jake said as he pulled into the alleyway behind the shop. "Don't go in empty-handed. There's a lot to bring in and set up." He turned to her. "That wasn't for you. You don't have to help."

"I'm happy to do my share." She opened the door before he could come around and get it for her. She didn't need him near her, to smell his cologne, or any other reason to want to take him down a secluded bookstore aisle to get lost in his kisses. She needed a man less than another panic attack. The problem was, she hadn't had a man in her life for years. The last time she could remember being with anyone was when she was twenty-seven and working at Tipsy's in Sacramento. She couldn't remember the guy's name. Not sure she'd even asked. It was a one-night thing. Kind of like taking a throat lozenge to ease the pain. Once it was gone, it was forgotten.

She grabbed the crayons and markers along with the cardstock and kids' scissors. She considered how brave it was to allow scissors and markers in a bookstore. She hoped Jake knew what he was getting himself into.

They made several trips back and forth until the cargo area was empty, and a sheen of sweat covered their brows.

Jake looked at his watch and then at her. "Would you mind watching the counter for a few minutes?" He pointed to his watch. "I've got a conference call in ten minutes."

She narrowed her eyes. "Was this your plan all along, your way of getting me to run your register?"

His eyes shifted to look at the ceiling. "Yep, I caused

you to have a panic attack, broke your car, and covered your shifts so you could be here just in case."

"Thought so." She stuck her tongue out at him.

He stared for several seconds. First at her tongue, then at her lips.

"Is that a yes, you'll help?"

"Show me what to do."

He showed her how to scan the book in for inventory and then told her to calculate the discount and ring it up on the old register.

"Got it. Go change the world."

"That's my plan. World domination—one person at a time." He leaned in as if he would kiss her, but he caught himself mid lunge and turned the other way.

She moved around the corner to unlock the door and flip the closed sign to open.

For a small town, there was consistent traffic to the bookstore. The first person in was Cannon.

"Hey, Natalie. I didn't know you worked here." He moved past her to the self-help section before she could correct him.

Five minutes later, he peeked his head around the shelf. "Do you know where the book *What to Expect When You're Expecting* is?"

She rounded the counter and considered his question. The bookstore was too small to have a parenting section, but maybe it was in the non-fiction area. Having been down the rows several times, she knew exactly where to look.

"I'd assume it's in non-fiction." She moved through the books until she found what he was looking for. "Here you go." She considered asking if he and Sage were trying for a baby, but thought it was too personal a question.

"Sage is convinced she won't be ready when our little lima bean is born."

*What the hell?* "Are you pregnant or still practicing?"

He looked at her like she'd grown a third eye. "She's due around Thanksgiving." He skimmed through the book. "I guess you weren't here when we made the announcement."

"No, I was probably picking up Will." She glanced at the shelf and saw a familiar face looking back at her. The book by Jake was called *Love the Life You Live.* She tucked it to her side and walked Cannon to the register, where she hid it on the ledge below. "Isn't she a neonatal nurse? I thought for sure she'd have this motherhood stuff down pat." She took the book from him and scanned it.

"I guess it's different when it's yours."

"Do you need anything else?"

"Nope. That should do it. Unless they have reference material on how to be a supportive husband without wanting to kill your baby mama."

She took the twenty and made change. "Maybe you should write that one after you survive. Could be a bestseller."

"Maybe I will." He shoved his change into his front pocket. "If I survive."

"You two will be great."

Cannon walked out, and she pulled the book from under the counter, opening it to the first chapter, called, "The things we avoid are the things we grow the most from."

She read how most people isolate themselves from their past hurts to avoid future pain, but they limit their existence and can't lead an authentic life.

She scanned the chapter headings.

"Negative thoughts—you can't stop them from entering your head, but you can refuse to let them take up residence in your life."

She scrolled down the list, stopping on the ones that jumped out at her like, "Fear regret more than failure," and "Progress involves risk; you can't move forward if you don't take the first step."

She was fully engrossed when her phone pinged with an incoming message.

**Hi,**

**This is Lydia. Hope it's okay that Doc gave me your number, but I wanted to let you know that Wes has a house that might work for you. It's on Pansy Lane. Let me know when you'll be in town to see it.**

**Lydia**

She closed the book and placed it back under the counter. She shut her eyes and said a silent prayer of hope before she texted back.

**I'm at the bookstore helping. What are the terms?**

**Natalie**

There was no use in getting her hopes up if she couldn't afford it.

An answer came back immediately.

**Work, like painting and gardening for rent. It's not updated yet, but it's got everything you'll need.**

She bounced on her toes. Could it be real, or was this another way the universe would give her the finger? She tamped down her excitement and replied.

**Is there any way I can see it today?**

Lydia didn't text back. Instead, she walked into the bookstore a few minutes later and handed her a set of keys.

"Wes said to let him know. If you want the place, keep the keys, and start moving your stuff over. If not, bring them back to the clinic. I'll be there all day." She turned to leave. "Did you get word on your car?"

Natalie shook her head. "No, and I'm afraid to ask."

"Doc said he'd take care of it and he will. I've never seen him promise something and renege." She looked to where Will was setting up a Lego table in the corner. "Can I borrow him? We had a cancelation today, and I can fit in his physical and immunizations before our next patient."

Her first instinct was to say no because as nice as it sounded, it also meant that she'd be in debt to Doc and Lydia. Then again, wasn't she already? Soon, she'd have to file payback bankruptcy.

"Will, Doctor Lydia wants to take you for your school physical."

He eyed them both with apprehension. "Am I getting shots?"

"Do you have a shot record that shows your existing shots?"

"No." He shook his head. "But I'm sure my old school does."

"Good thinking. We'll start with the physical part. Agatha can call the school so they can fax over his shot records." She pulled open the door. "Let's go, buddy. If you're good, you can steal a candy bar from Doc's shelf."

Will's eyes nearly popped from his head. "I gave that up. I've been a member of shoplifters anonymous since I moved in with my sister, the warden."

She raced around the counter to give him a pinch, but Will was too quick and was out the door before she could reach him.

Another thirty minutes went by before Jake walked out of the office.

"How did it go?" He looked around. "Where's my partner?"

"Lydia picked him up and took him for his school physical and shots."

"Ouch." Jake moved around to the back of the register.

"Yep, doesn't sound fun at all."

When Jake leaned down, she knew he would see the book she'd been reading. She rushed to grab it before he did but was once again too slow.

"Can't get enough of me, huh?" He moved closer. The smell of his cologne filled her nostrils with its intoxicating scent. It wasn't overwhelming—just the perfect blend of man and sex appeal.

"Give me that." She reached for the book.

He shook his head slowly and moved in closer until he'd pinned her against the wall. "Not a chance. You want to talk about the book, or share another kiss we shouldn't but know we will? While I know it's not wise, I can't resist you, and I don't think you can resist me either."

"You're confident." She set her hands on his chest, ready to push him back, but she let her fingers float over the cotton to feel each hill and valley.

"More like perceptive. I'm great at reading people, and while your body language is primed to push me away, the deeper green of your eyes and the pulse of your artery at the base of your neck says something altogether different." He ran his fingers from her cheek to the pulse point at the sensitive crook.

"What you think you see is my excitement over a home for Will and me. If you can watch the register for yourself, I'll walk over and see if it will do."

He set his hand on her shoulders. "Darn, I was hoping you wanted that kiss. I've been dreaming about another one since yesterday. Those lips have other skills than spitting out sass."

"You're impossible." She flattened her hands on his chest, getting ready to shove, but she gripped his shirt and pulled him in for that kiss they'd both been craving. Just as his lips were touching hers, the door opened and in walked Will.

"Doctors suck. And shots are worse."

Jake jumped back. He pulled something from her hair. "There it is. Not a spider but lint." He dropped nothing into her hand and winked.

"You were kissing my sister."

"He was looking ..." She stopped mid-sentence. She would lie, but that was against the rules. In her book, it was all right to lie to herself but not to others.

"For your tonsils?" Will looked between them and grinned. "Took you long enough. I'm only twelve, and even I see more action than you."

Jake ignored Will's comment. "You ready to go see that house?"

Will's demeanor brightened. "There's a house? Can I go?"

"We're all going." Jake flipped the sign to closed.

"Everyone will think you're closed more than you're open." She stepped around him and swiped the keys from the counter.

Jake shrugged. "Until I find an employee, the hours will vary according to my needs. Putting myself first doesn't mean I'm putting anyone last. Right now, I'm seeing to you and Will because you two are important to me."

The heat of his words warmed her chest while the memory of touching him made other parts of her downright sizzle.

"You are leaving, right?" she asked as she led the way to the back door. "You know, you're temporary, correct?"

"That's the plan."

"Perfect."

She climbed inside the SUV and smiled. Maybe she needed a lozenge named Jake to take care of the ache inside her.

"What's the address?" Jake pulled out of the alleyway and turned toward Main Street.

She looked at the tag on the keys. "Thirty-five Pansy Lane. Take the first right and then a left." She leaned toward the dash to get the first glimpse of what could be their home. "I could have walked."

Jake smiled. "You could have, but I wanted to see it too."

"There." She pointed to the house in the center of a weed garden. The paint was peeling, and the picket fence that surrounded the yard was missing several pickets, but it had a roof, and the porch wasn't being held up with a wedged-in two by four. On her initial glance, it had windows.

"It's a fixer-upper," Jake said while parking at the curb.

"It looks haunted," Will whispered.

"I'm sure it's not." She opened her door and stepped onto the patch of overgrown weeds that lined the street.

Jake and Will followed her through the squeaky gate and up the front steps. She stomped on the surface to make sure it wouldn't cave in. Or maybe it was a warning to any rodents living inside to vacate.

When she put in the key and turned the lock, she held her breath. What would wait on the other side?

As the door opened, she stood on the threshold, ready to bolt if something skittered her way. She could do spiders, but rats and mice were a no-go in her book.

When nothing charged forward, she inched inside. The house was dusty and smelled stale, but there weren't any holes in the living room floor, and the lights were attached to the ceilings.

She let out a sigh of relief.

Will brushed past her, wincing when his arm grazed hers. "Holy smokes." He painfully spread his just immunized arms and turned in a circle. "There's so much room."

She moved through the room while Will ran down a hallway, no doubt to pick out his bedroom. She walked into the kitchen and stood in front of the sink. The space was galley style with white speckled counters and harvest-gold appliances.

"Let's cross our fingers."

Jake stood behind her as she reached for the faucet and turned the knob. When clear water rushed out, she giggled with glee.

She turned around and wrapped her arms around his waist. "It's perfect. Oh. My. God. It's perfect."

"I suppose it's all perspective."

"I want it. I need it."

109

He leaned down and brushed his lips across hers. "You're saying, yes?"

"Yes," she shouted.

"About the house or our next kiss?"

He didn't give her a moment to process the question. Instead, he covered her mouth with his and made her feel things she hadn't felt in years or since the last kiss he'd given her.

She told herself that it wasn't him that made her heart race and her insides smolder; it was the excitement of having a house, but she knew she wasn't being honest. Jake could be hazardous to her heart if he stayed, but knowing he would leave allowed her to take a risk and be self-indulgent.

"I picked out my room," Will said as he raced around the corner and stopped dead beside them.

Jake didn't jump back this time. He finished the kiss and then turned around to smile. "That's awesome."

Will tried to keep his grin from growing, but he was twelve and had no self-control.

"Oh, don't stop for me. A kid could learn a lot by watching."

"Go to your room," she said and pulled Jake down for another kiss.

# CHAPTER TWELVE

Jake wanted to toss the phone across the room. "You're bringing in another candidate?" he asked Matt Steinman.

"You've got nothing to worry about. Out of the three, I like you the best, but sadly we have a board of directors. Since a partnership is a long-term relationship, the board wants to make sure it will last."

"Might as well just bring everyone to Vision Quest and have a coach off. Kind of like a *Chopped* championship for life coaches, just to see what secret techniques and ingredients we have in our basket."

"Not a bad idea."

"I was being flippant, Matt. I got the impression this was a done deal when the offer letter came in." He held back the growl building in his throat.

"You didn't sign it."

He closed his eyes and clenched his jaw. After a count of three, he exhaled. "I told you I needed to tie up loose ends, and I couldn't commit to a specific date until I was certain I had everything in order."

"Is it in order?"

"Almost."

He looked around the bookstore at the rows of colorful spines. He breathed in the scent of paper mixed with the lemon-infused furniture polish used on the tables at the end of the day. He'd miss the bookstore and Will. His heart lurched when he thought of Natalie. He'd miss her the most.

"Get your ducks in a row, man. We need you here."

"You don't need me. You need someone with deep pockets and my skill set."

Matt ignored the statement. "I'll keep you posted."

He hung up and looked at his schedule. He'd been in Aspen Cove for weeks longer than he expected. Doc was certain once the shop was opened, there would be a line of people waiting to interview. The only application he'd gotten was from Louise, who was nice enough, but when she said she'd have to bring her eight kids to work with her, he passed. That was opening day and two weeks ago.

As much as he shouldn't care what happened after he left, he did. Building the shop was a labor of love. Love for a woman he'd never met but who gave him the greatest gift since his mother birthed him.

The door opened, and Will walked inside, looking bedraggled with smudges of dirt coloring his cheeks.

"Look at you. Did you give up the bookstore and find another career path?" He opened the small refrigerator from under the counter to get Will a bottle of water. "Drink this and take a seat. Tell me what you're up to." He knew what Will was up to. Natalie had texted to tell him not to pick them up because they had gotten a ride from Tilden, who was coming into town early, and she wanted to get a head start on the cleanup.

He'd missed seeing them first thing in the morning.

112

"She's working me to death."

"You'll live. Remember that she's doing this for you. There's sacrifice to every gain."

"I don't even know what that means." Will drank deeply.

"It means that often, the important stuff takes work. Your sacrifice is hard labor. Your sister's is much bigger. She's working beside you, on top of taking on the responsibility of a house and raising a brilliant young man."

Will always thrived under positive reinforcement. Since his arrival, Jake had watched Will transform from a thug-in-training to a young man with a bright future.

With the dramatic flair that only a boy could have, Will dropped his head to the table with a thunk. "It doesn't take any brains to clean, and if Wes brings over the leftover paint he used on his house, then I'll be painting until I keel over." He lifted his head. "Why can't we hire a painter?"

"You can, but that might mean you can't eat for the week."

"Not true. You gave us more food than we know what to do with."

That sparked an idea. "How about I get Agatha to watch things, and I come over to help?"

Will jumped up. "Now that's an idea." He looked at the clock hanging on the wall. "I better get going, or she'll send out a search party."

"Why are you here?"

A hint of red painted his cheeks. "I'm supposed to get my shot records, so Nat has a copy of them, and then come right back."

"Nat?"

His smile spread wide. "Yeah, she thinks it's a term of

endearment—a nickname, but I call her that because she's like the bug."

"Which starts with a G."

Will rose from the chair. "That's why I get away with it. She doesn't ask me to spell it." He turned toward the door, and before he opened it, he said, "Just so you know, I think you're brilliant, too." Will raced out and down the street.

Jake was on the phone seconds later.

"Agatha, I know you don't technically work here, but could you cover the rest of the day? I want to help Natalie get the house ready."

There was a pause and some muffled chatter as if she'd covered the phone.

"I'll be right over."

She showed up five minutes later with a jumbo bag of Skittles and a Red Bull.

"Those drinks will kill you if the candy doesn't do it first."

She dismissed him with a wave. "I gave up gambling, drinking, and sex, on most days. This is my new vice."

He didn't want to remind her that she enjoyed a glass of wine nightly at Bishop's Brewhouse. As far as the sex, he wouldn't go there with a septuagenarian.

"Thank you for doing this. Natalie could use the help."

She settled onto the stool behind the counter. "And you look like you could use Natalie."

"You might be right." He left through the front door. It was just after noon, and he was certain neither Natalie nor Will had eaten, so he stopped at the diner for burgers and fries for them and a grilled chicken breast salad for himself.

He took a seat at the counter and watched as Maisey and Louise tamed the lunch crowd.

When Louise leaned against the back bar for a breather, Jake said, "Thanks for covering for Natalie."

"It's a blessing to me. I could use the work. With five out of my eight kids heading for school, things are tight. Don't get me wrong. We aren't hungry or anything. It's more about the school supplies and clothes. Brian wears out a pair of sneakers every few months. Eric is growing like a weed. He's the second oldest, but he's inches taller than Brian, and only a few short of Bobby. Don't get me started on the girls. The hair ties alone could send me to debtor's prison."

"Where are the kids now?"

She gave him a devious smile. "I duct-taped them to the wall." She covered her mouth to squelch the laughter. "Just kidding." She nodded toward the table where Will usually sat. Shoved into the booth were six of her eight. "Bobby's sister is keeping an eye on the babies. She can't handle them all."

"Order up," Ben called from the window.

Maisey rushed over to grab it.

As Jake pulled cash from his pocket, and Louise rushed off to refill coffees and sodas, he asked, "Would you miss Natalie too much if she were to leave the diner?"

Maisey cocked her head. "Are you taking her with you?" She put her pen to her mouth and gnawed on the end. "I heard rumors about you two."

"No, and we're just friends." He glanced around the diner. "I was thinking about how Louise needs stable employment to keep her kids in shoes. And although she applied for the job at the bookstore, I don't think having the kids there would be good for the business."

"Or good for the books." Maisey handed him the bill and swiped up both twenties he offered. As she made change at the nearby register, she asked, "You want Natalie to manage the bookstore?" The cash drawer opened with a ding and closed with a thud. "She depends on the steady influx of daily cash." She put his change on the counter.

He hadn't considered that. "What do you think she makes?"

Maisey laughed. "I can tell you what she makes. It's not enough to retire on, and just enough to get by."

"Seriously, Maisey. If I can steal her from you, I need to offer something enticing. Now that she has Will, she'll need a stable paycheck." He knew waitressing wouldn't provide that. One massive storm could stop her income flow for days.

Maisey frowned. "While I hate to lose her because she's so good, if you could convince her to leave so Louise could take her job, and you provided her with a livable wage, I'd make the sacrifice. Letting her go would help the greater good."

"I agree. Let me see what I can do." He grabbed the bag and turned toward the door.

"Hey, you forgot your change."

He chuckled. "Put it into your retirement account."

As he drove to 35 Pansy Lane, he realized how perfect this plan was. The house was conveniently located close to the bookstore. While it was the same for the diner, managing the shop gave her more flexibility. No one would be disconcerted if it was closed, so she could take Will to school or grab lunch at the diner.

With the bags of food in his hands, he walked toward the open door. Gone was the dust-covered floor, and in its place worn but clean planks of oak. The air smelled of Pine-Sol instead of mustiness.

"In the kitchen," Natalie said.

He walked in and found her halfway inside the oven. The lower half stuck out and wiggled as she scrubbed.

He could have stood there all day and watched her round bottom move, but that would defeat his purpose of coming to help.

"I brought food."

"I smell burgers," Will called from the living room. He raced toward the kitchen and slid to a stop in the doorway. "Are you staring at my sister's—"

"You want that cheeseburger or not, buddy?" He gave him a side-eye.

Natalie shimmied back and stood. "You were watching my—"

"Hard to ignore," he cut in. "Now, come and eat." He looked around and noticed there was no place for them to sit. "Let's go outside." He led them to the porch, where they took a seat on the steps. "Will, please go to the SUV and get three water bottles."

Will slogged toward the gate now propped open with a large rock.

"If you'd told him there was soda in the car, he'd already be back." She peeked inside the first bag. "This is for you." She pulled out the salad and plastic utensils. "You didn't have to bring us lunch. I brought a loaf of bread and a jar of peanut butter. We would have been okay."

"I know, but I wanted to see you." He reached over and wiped a smudge of black grease from her chin. "You're a mess, and yet you're still beautiful."

She lowered her head, but the blush reached her ears.

"Catch," Will said just before he lobbed the water bottles like missiles in their direction.

Luckily for them, they were quick to respond, or else they'd both be out cold or at least bruised.

"Next time, you hand them over nicely," Natalie reprimanded. "You could have hurt us."

A loud sigh escaped. "Sorry. I was trying to have some fun."

"It's okay. Let's eat and do more cleaning, and maybe we can persuade Jake to take us for ice cream."

Will shifted his lips from side to side. "That's not fun. That's just tasty."

"You haven't been to Sam's Scoops. His truck sits next to a park around the lake, and he serves up interesting ice cream flavors."

Will opened the bag and pulled out his burger and fries. He was about to shove a bite in his mouth and stopped. "Interesting how?"

She giggled, and it was a beautiful sound.

"Things like green tea and grasshopper guts or dog bones and dynamite."

"Grasshopper guts?" Jake asked.

"Not really. It's just a name, but it's a fun one."

"Let's eat and finish up cleaning so we can go eat guts and dog bones."

"I'm in," Will said and bit into his burger.

Natalie opened her Styrofoam container and pulled the onion off the burger. She leaned over and whispered, "In case you want to kiss me again."

"You think onions will stop me?" He looked at Will. "Care if I kiss your sister?"

"You didn't ask for permission the first time." Ketchup

oozed from the corner of his mouth until he cleaned it up with a swipe of his tongue.

"You're right." He handed Will a napkin. "Occasionally, I'd like to kiss your sister and stuff. Is that okay?"

Will rolled his eyes. "I don't mind the kissing, but I don't want to see the 'and stuff.' I got eyefuls of that when my dad was alive, and some crack ho came to get her fix."

How this boy ever made it out alive was a mystery. "Duly noted."

As they finished their lunch, a truck pulled to the curb. Wes Covington got out and reached into the bed to grab gallons of paint. They hung from his fingers like ornaments from a tree. The cans swayed back and forth on his walk to the porch.

"Afternoon." Wes set them on the porch. "I went through the paint and found these. I've got two more gallons at home if you need them." He popped the top off to show a soft beige.

Natalie jumped from her place on the steps and threw her arms around him. "Thank you so much. I ... I don't know how to thank you."

"You just did." Looking uncomfortable with the show of affection, Wes stepped back and shoved his hands inside his pockets. "I swiped up all the houses I could before Mason Van der Veen did. This is one of the better ones, but with the high demand for skilled workers, it will be a while before I can get to it." He smiled. "You're doing me a favor. Vacant properties seem to fall apart faster than occupied homes."

"Can't I pay you something?"

"You are. You're painting." He turned in a circle. "And if you can beat this yard into submission, I'd be grateful."

Will stood and wiped his hands on his jeans before holding his out. "Thank you, Mr. Wes. This sure makes up for all the times your wife poked me with a needle."

Wes laughed. "That's her superpower. Stay on her good side, or the next ones will hurt worse." He said his goodbyes and drove off.

"Break's over." Natalie stood and gathered the garbage.

Jake quickly ate the rest of his salad and followed her into the house. "Where do you want me?"

She lifted a brow. "Where do I want you, or where do I need you?" She shook her head, and her whole body appeared to shudder. "Seeing as they're both the same, how about you focus on the windows?" She moved into the kitchen and picked up the spray bottle of cleaner and a roll of paper towels.

"I've got a better idea. How about you finish the oven, and I'll supervise from behind?"

She pointed to the living room. "Out."

They scrubbed and cleaned until half-past four. When the broom fell from her hands, and she looked ready to seep into the hardwood floors, he yelled for Will. "Time for grasshopper guts."

Natalie wiped her brow with the back of her hand. "I don't know if I have the energy for that."

"All you need to do is sit in the car. I'll do the rest."

Will ran from the hallway to the SUV without further coaxing.

Jake wrapped his arm around Natalie and gave her a squeeze. "You've done well."

She tilted her head up to see him. "I hope it's enough."

NATALIE FELL asleep on the thirty-minute drive. When he stopped in front of Sam's Scoops Ice Cream truck, he told Will to go pick what he wanted, and he'd be there to pay in a few minutes.

"Hey love, we're here." He leaned over and gave her a gentle kiss.

Her eyes fluttered open, and she groaned. "Oh my God, I feel like I've experienced some kind of medieval torture."

"No rack or guillotine present, but how about an ice cream?"

Immediately, she appeared to have more energy. "Sounds great, but I'm buying."

He'd never let her pay. Her stubborn sense of pride was why he didn't hire someone to come in and do the work for her. She wouldn't have allowed it. But ice cream ... she'd have to live with him buying her a cup or cone.

He exited the car and rushed over to open her door. Instead of letting her walk, he scooped her into his arms.

"What are you doing?" she squealed.

"I told you all you had to do was sit. I'm a man of my word." He carried her to the empty picnic bench.

Will ran over. The excitement oozed from his pores. "They have three flavors." He raised his hand and made a face. "There's something called Tie Me Up, which is red rope licorice and strawberry ice cream. Snots and Dots, which is vanilla ice cream with caramel syrup and chocolate sprinkles, and then there is what I'm having."

It was hard not to get excited with him looking ready to burst out of his skin. "What's that?"

"Dinosaur Dung."

"Gross." Natalie made a gagging sound. "You wouldn't eat black bean soup, but you'll eat dinosaur poop?"

"It's not really poop. It's chocolate ice cream with brownie bites dipped in rock candy, so it looks like meteor bits."

"Sounds ... amazing." She reached in her back pocket and took out a twenty. "I'm paying."

"Not a chance. What will it be?"

Knowing she wouldn't win, she quickly gave up. "Snots and dots."

Will took his cone to a nearby swing set while Jake sat across from Natalie eating his Tie Me Up minus the licorice.

"This should give me enough energy to pack up a few things when we get home. Would you mind swinging by to pick us up in the morning?"

She licked the cone. Each time her tongue swept up the cream, his body twitched with need.

"Not a problem. Do you need my help packing your stuff? I don't have plans tonight."

She considered his offer for a moment. "No, you've already done enough for me. I hate to ask for the ride, but it's too far to walk, and I'd like to get started on the painting tomorrow." She took another lick. "I called Bobby about my car, and he said it was a bad alternator. I feel bad because I know things are tight with them, and he has to pay for the part up-front." She gripped her cone so hard it fractured and fell to the table, leaving what little bit of ice cream was left on her palm.

He took her hand and raised it to his mouth, licking off the stickiness. The whole time their eyes never left each other's. It was the deepest sense of intimacy he'd felt with a woman, and he wasn't even inside her. When all the stickiness was gone, he kissed her palm and set it down on the table.

"I have a proposition for you."

She looked down at her hand. "Does it include your tongue?"

"It could, but this isn't sexual. It's responsible."

She let out a *bleh*. "I'm so tired of adulting."

"Just hear me out. You're right, Bobby and Louise are struggling, and it will only get worse as their kids grow older. You see how much Will costs, and they have eight children."

Natalie buried her head in her hands. "I can't imagine. I wish I could pay Bobby for the part. Doc said he'd take care of it, but I'm not sure what that means. Is it a trade of some sort?"

"I don't know, but I know how you can help. Quit the diner and come to work at the bookshop." When she was about to say no, he held up his hand. "Listen, before you argue. Louise can work at Maisey's and bring her kids like you do Will, but that's not possible at the bookstore. We'll end up with lots of bindings and no pages. I really need someone to take over B's Book Nook." He took a breath and continued. "You can set your own hours, and close when you need to for weather, illness, or to watch Will in the school play. I've set aside funding for a decent annual salary, so you don't have to depend on tips. You'd have a consistent paycheck that would allow you some extras." He did his best to sell her on the idea, but he wasn't sure he had.

"I didn't realize Louise had applied for the job. Now I feel selfish; her husband is working for free to fix my piece of junk. Today it's the alternator and with my luck the starter tomorrow, and the battery by the weekend."

"Hey." He lifted her chin. "Don't borrow trouble. If you take the job, you'll make enough to pay for your own repairs next time."

"You're relentless in your attempt to pawn the shop off on someone so you can go." The corners of her mouth drooped into a frown.

"I thought that you liked me because I was temporary."

"It's the best thing about you ... and your kisses." She lifted from her seat and pressed a kiss to his lips. "Now, tell me about my salary and benefits."

# CHAPTER THIRTEEN

"I'm not a freeloader." She moved around the bookstore pushing in chairs and straightening books.

"I know you're not, but I thought you'd want to work on the house this week." Jake followed her into the fiction aisle where a box of books sat on the floor, waiting for her to shelve them. "You don't have much time before the next home visit."

She frowned, knowing what he said was true, but she had to do what she felt was right, and working her shift was right. "Are these already entered into the system?" She moved several books to the side to make room for the new Grisham novels. It turned out the people of Aspen Cove liked conflict and angst after all, but in books and not their lives.

"Yes." He stopped her hand mid progress. "Natalie. You don't have to show up to work until you have the house ready."

"I do." She pulled away and touched her hand to her chest. "I have a lot of pride. Maybe too much. I've never had so much at once, and I need to feel like I'm earning my keep. Besides, I can't be without a paycheck for weeks on end." She didn't want to admit that without the food he put in her house, they would eat canned beans and crackers each night. "I need this. Let me do what I have to in order to get things done."

He bent over and picked up the stack of books. "Fine, but you have to have a balance. I can give you an advance." His eyes lit up. "Oh, I know ... what about a sign-on bonus?"

"Haven't you done enough?"

The door to the shop opened, and she rushed to the front where she found Mercy Meyer leaning on the counter. She wasn't in her normal sweater set and slacks. Today she wore a pink sundress that showed off her assets —especially when said assets were trapped together between her arms.

"Oh, hi." Mercy bolted up and stepped back, adjusting the neckline of her dress up. "I was ..." Her head cocked to the side with a perplexed expression. She lifted on her tiptoes and craned her neck to see over Natalie. "Is Jake here?"

She swallowed the ill-placed jealousy. It was a stupid emotion since Jake wasn't hers and never would be. They both knew the kisses they shared meant nothing. It was a nice distraction from the stress of their everyday lives.

"Jake," she called.

He peeked around the bookshelf and smiled. "Mercy, good to see you." He arrived at the counter in less than a dozen steps. "I bet you're here to see if I got those Eric Litwin books in."

She blushed and leaned forward. Once again, Mercy's assets were on display, and Natalie watched with interest.

"Yes, but also ..." She turned toward Natalie and smiled. "Maybe she can get the books while I discuss something of a personal nature with you."

Having spent a solid amount of time with Jake over the last few weeks, it was fun to watch him respond to her not so subtle adoration.

"Where would I find them?" she asked Jake. "I don't want to be an interloper to a private conversation." She went to slide by Jake, but he grabbed her hand and tugged her back.

"Nothing to interrupt." He glanced at her quickly, but in those few seconds, she saw the *Help me* embedded in his blue irises. "Natalie manages the store now, so anything you have to say to me should be said to Natalie since she'll be taking care of things from this point forward."

He tugged her close, so they touched on one side. It was as if he was pushing the point of solidarity. But Natalie knew by the look in Mercy's eyes that she wasn't here about the books. She also imagined what the not so schoolmarm-ish teacher wanted couldn't be delegated to another. She wanted Jake.

"Umm, I ..." Mercy squirmed in front of the counter. "Honestly ..." She inhaled and let out a whoosh. When she grew an inch taller and pulled back her shoulders, she said, "I'd like to have lunch with you."

Jake stood like a statue, looking at her without so much as a blink. If his jaw hadn't ticked or the arm hanging between them hadn't twitched, she could have believed it stunned him to stone.

Natalie bumped him with her hip to get him to respond. "Mercy would like to take you to lunch."

Jake shook his head. "That's so nice of you, but

honestly, there is so much that Natalie and I have to cover before I leave, that it's impossible to free up the time." It all came out in a single string of words without a breath or a break in the sentence.

She wanted to laugh at him for being so nervous. Here was a confident life coach, and he was faltering. Part of her wanted to tease him for it; the other part wanted to take him behind the stacks and kiss him. Mercy Meyer was beautiful and willing, and he wasn't interested.

No doubt it was because he was leaving, but she wanted to believe that it was her. She was enough for him.

A giggle slipped from her, and both Jake and Mercy turned to stare. Mercy's was more of a glower.

"That's right. I forgot about our lunch meeting." Taking a step sideways to gain some distance, she added, "But Mr. Powers is free now for tea." She moved around the corner and walked straight to the door. "He likes the decaf variety."

Mercy's expression went from downtrodden to lottery win happy. "Tea would work. Although I'm not a fan, I can have coffee."

With the door held open, she waved them out. Jake stood at the counter for a long minute before he gave in. As he passed her, he leaned in and whispered, "You will pay for this."

"I'll look forward to our meeting, Mr. Powers."

That thread of jealousy wasn't there when they walked out because he wasn't interested in Mercy.

She moved back to the stacks and stocked the shelves. Thirty minutes later, she was standing at the counter scanning in the Patterson books when Jake returned. He immediately turned over the open sign to closed.

"I'd like to see you in your office, please." He moved past her at a fast clip while she stared after him.

Had she pushed things too far? She'd never seen him riled up or upset, but his curt direction led her to believe that maybe she'd driven him to anger.

She set the book down and marched into the room after him. As she neared the door, she said, "I'm sorry. I thought it was funny to see you squirm." As she passed the threshold, he yanked her inside and slammed the door.

"You're sorry?"

Within seconds he'd pinned her to the wall, his body so close that she could feel the heat emanating from him.

"Yes."

"Do you want me to date Mercy while I'm here?" He penetrated her with his blue eyes. Eyes that somehow had fire in them despite their cool ocean-blue color.

"No, I ..."

"You what?" He leaned in and brushed his nose across her cheek until he reached her ear. "Is that your thing? You like competition?"

She shook her head, but his mouth stayed close to her ear. "Are you protecting yourself?" he whispered. "Pushing me away, so when I leave, it's not a loss?"

His breath sent shivers all the way down her spine. She tried to push back, but there was no way to get beyond the wall pressing hard against her spine.

"No, of course not. We know what this is. This is an attraction run amuck, but it means nothing."

He moved until his lips were against hers. "Yep, that's what I told myself too until you tossed me out the door with another woman. Now I intend to prove otherwise. This might go nowhere, but dammit, it means something."

He kissed her hard and rough as if he meant to brand her. She'd been telling herself that it meant nothing, that his kisses were a way to reward herself for surviving another day, but was he right?

His body molded around hers like a warm blanket. His presence was reassuring, his passion exciting, his kisses—everything. His nearness fogged her sensibilities. Somehow in the course of a few weeks, she'd gone from being an island adrift to an anchored peninsula. The anchor being Jake Powers. Her heart said finally, but her head screamed at her to step back and gain perspective. *Don't let a few kisses steal your good sense.* A heart was simply an organ to keep her alive, not a litmus test to determine her value.

As she pondered the value of giving in to the moment, her heart beat faster. The rush of blood ringing in her ears drowned out the sensible advice of her brain and subconscious.

Jake was right: this meant something. It meant she was lonely and hungry. Hungry for attention and affection. Jake had made it a point to feed her, so why not let him nourish those parts too?

Her hands moved up his body to thread through his hair. She tugged the roots to pull him closer—to get her fill. She might not have him for long, but she'd overindulge while she did. She pulled back and said, "Eat your heart out, Mercy Meyer. This man belongs to me." *For now.*

"That's my girl." He stepped back and pulled her with him down to the floor. The hardwood couldn't have been comfortable for him, but she didn't have to feel it. The only thing hard beneath her was his arousal. The rest was a bed of muscles that her body melted into.

They kissed like they were both starved. He tasted like sweet mint, which was probably the tea he'd had with Mercy. After the first five minutes of frenzied kisses, things slowed, with his velvet tongue exploring her mouth like he was Lewis and Clark and her mouth the new world. His expedition was thorough. When his hands joined in, every skin cell sang hallelujah.

Jake had a gentle touch, but she knew he was capable of more. If his hands had followed the lead of his mouth, she'd be naked on the floor of the office right now.

He ended the kiss and bracketed her head with his hands, pushing her away enough so they could see eye to eye. "You're beautiful."

She shook her head. "Not really. I'm just me."

"And I think you're perfect."

Those words caused a giggle to erupt in her belly, tickling her insides until it turned into a full laugh. She moved so much she rolled off his body and came down onto the floor beside him.

"For a life coach, you sure are unobservant. I'm far from perfection."

"It depends on the rubric you're using."

She hadn't thought about it in that way. At thirty, perspective was everything. Age gave you more, but so did experiences. "You're using a flexible curve when grading, and your expectations must be low."

He sat up and scooted to the desk to lean against it. "Come here," he said and held out his hand. "It's time you got to know me a little, but first, I want to tell you things you might not know about yourself."

She moved beside him.

As one of the most self-reflective people she knew,

there wasn't anything Jake could tell her she didn't already know.

"Okay, tell me, Mr. Almighty and Wise, who am I, and what don't I know?"

He turned to face her. "You're fearless."

"Wrong. I'm scared of everything."

"But you do things regardless, and that makes you fearless. Or maybe the only thing you fear is fear itself." He cupped her cheek. "You're selfless."

She laughed. "Wrong again. I'm selfish. I don't allow people into my life because I don't want to share."

He shook his head slowly, a sparkle of amusement twinkling in his eyes. "That's what you tell yourself, but really, you open yourself up to a lot of things. Like your brother. Or this new job. It takes time to learn about things and people. You're doing it."

He had her all wrong. "I'm all about what's necessary. I do what I have to, to survive."

"You can lie to yourself again, but I know your truth. You're scared to admit that you love because love is painful. But it's also powerful. Yes, you hold back just enough so that if love disappoints you, you won't disappear along with it. But you know what, the only person you're hurting is yourself. You can't really fully love anyone until you love yourself, and that's where you're hung up. Someone once told you and showed you, you were not worthy or lovable, but it's not true. I think you're easy to love. Who wouldn't love a woman who'd drive across the country to save a kid? You're relentless in your desire to keep Will. A lesser person would have let the foster care system swallow him up."

"I'd never!" she shouted. "I've been there, and it's not

always great. It's a crapshoot. You get the hand you're dealt, and mine sucked."

"And despite all that, you survived." He moved his hand from her cheek to the scruff on his face. "If I were creating life success teams, I'd want you on mine."

"That's very nice, but don't let my ability to adapt fool you. It's a defense mechanism. I become who I have to, to endure. I'm like a chameleon."

He wrapped his arm around her waist and pulled her into his lap. "I like your colors." He pressed a gentle kiss to her lips. "And I love this mouth."

The heat of passion coiled tighter and became hotter with every touch of his lips. Too bad he wasn't staying in Aspen Cove because a girl didn't need to eat if her lunch hour was filled with his kisses.

As his hand moved in to cup her breast, a loud pounding sounded from the back door.

"Natalie, are you in there?" Will called out and pounded again.

Jake groaned. "We could ignore him. I was just getting to the good stuff."

She pulled herself up and stood looking down. "You call that the good stuff?" It was good, but the kisses and feels weren't enough.

He grabbed the edge of the desk and hauled himself to his feet. "That's the good stuff before we get to the *really* good stuff."

# CHAPTER FOURTEEN

Two days later and Jake could still feel her lips against his. Still imagine the weight of her breast in his palm. Two days that he hadn't had the pleasure of her touch, only her presence.

As much as Natalie wanted to fight him on her assessment, he knew he was right. She was fearless. She didn't shirk responsibilities or take them lightly. He made her the manager of B's Book Nook, and by the third day, she was running the shop like a well-oiled machine. She knew where everything was located from Tolstoy to Dr. Seuss. She didn't change the display weekly, but daily, so visitors always had something to look at. Her displays weren't static but interactive. She'd turned the spare iPad into a game for patrons. She filled it up with questions about the book or the author. It was Aspen Cove's version of trivia night.

He sat at the table and watched several of the regulars come in, as well as tourists, and pick up the book she was pushing for the day. It was the ones he'd overordered, and she sold them. She was holding a one to five ratio of interested patrons to sales, which was damn good. He'd have to add remarkable to his ever-growing list of descriptive words. So far, he had:

Beautiful

Resilient

Talented

Ambitious

Passionate

Brave

Creative

Modest

Protective

Proud

Guarded

Natalie was everything he'd find desirable in a woman.

He looked at his watch and dialed his next client. Her name was Marylin Richards, and she was a handful.

He tucked himself farther into the corner as he waited for her to answer.

Normally he would take the call in the office to afford him and his client privacy, but Natalie looked absolutely stunning today, and it made him feel good to just see her.

Mary picked up. "Oh, Dr. Powers, I'm so glad you called."

He shook his head. "Mary, I'm not a doctor. We've talked about this before. I have a master's degree in behavioral science, but I never attended medical school, nor did I continue on to get my Ph.D. Call me Jake."

Natalie looked at him and motioned to the office. He wasn't sure if she was suggesting he go or if she should, but he shook his head.

"Let's talk about your life and work balance." Mary

had taken on the job as a major pharmaceutical president, and it was more than she'd intended to bite off.

She made a phlegmy sound in her throat. "I've been eating that damn elephant one bite at a time like you said, but I'm so tired of elephant. I need something different."

Natalie leaned on the counter and stared at him. He often found her looking. Sometimes he didn't even need to see her eyes to know. The heat of her gaze was always warming his skin.

"Over the last six months, you've been telling me how miserable the place is. We've worked on your work and life balance."

"You've worked on my balance, but I'm still killing myself every day."

"Are you financially secure?"

"Yes, I'm set."

"So why stay?"

He waited for her to answer. He knew what she'd say, but it wasn't his job to fill in the blanks. The key to a good life coach was to help the client find the solution. He often set the pathway. Sometimes there were bright flashing lights that said *This way!* but ultimately, the person had to make the choice and own it.

"Because it's who I am. Without my job, I'd be no one."

That hit him like a slug to the heart. "You are not your job. Over the last few months, you've told me you have a husband named Clark and three beautiful kids; Sara, Todd, and Melanie, if I'm correct. You have a goldendoodle named Harry, and you belong to a book club that reads knitting cozies because you've always wanted to knit and don't have the time to do it yourself."

He glanced at Natalie, whose eyes had rounded to twice their size.

"I know, but this is the biggest thing about me."

"Not true. How did you start our conversation?" He could wait for her, but it was already said, so he repeated her statement about the elephant and how tired she was of eating it. "That's the biggest part of your life. How long do you want to eat that beast? And for what purpose? You don't need the money or the stress. Remember the saying *All work and no play makes Jack a dull boy?* Let's change it up. Stress is unhealthy. All work and no play makes Mary a dull woman, and possibly Clark a rich man when you kill yourself from overworking. Every hour has a value assigned to it. And only you know what that is. Make sure you know your return on investment. No one ever said *I wish I would have worked more* on their deathbed. At least I've never heard anyone."

There was a pause.

During the silence, he watched Natalie. She couldn't hear Mary's end of the conversation, but it seemed like she was soaking in his words.

"Are you telling me to quit?"

Inside, he wanted to yell, "Yes." However, the decision had to be hers. "I'm not telling you to do anything. What I'm saying is to listen to your inner voice. Let it guide you. It's the GPS you need to trust."

They discussed a few other issues before the call came to a close.

"Thanks, Jake, you are worth every penny I spend on you."

"Talk to you soon, Mary. Let me know what you decide."

"I will. If I quit, I can't afford you."

He chuckled. "I'll be okay." That wasn't a lie. He was wealthy by most standards. Not Getty or Kennedy wealthy, but he wouldn't ever starve. At three hundred dollars an hour, he did okay.

Once the call ended, he leaned back and closed his eyes. He made it a point to clear his head after each session because it served no one if he soaked up his clients' emotions and passed them on.

"Do you think she will?"

He opened his eyes and found Natalie standing in front of him. Under her chin was a smudge of beige paint. She'd rotated her shift to work on the house that morning and come in that afternoon so he could make his calls.

"Will she what?" He reached up and wiped at the paint, but it had dried hours ago and would be there until she washed it off.

"Quit."

"I was just trying to wipe off the paint," he said in his defense.

"What?" She touched the underside of her chin. "No, I didn't mean quit touching me." She blushed a pretty pink. "I meant, will she quit her job?"

He gathered his things and stood. "I don't know."

"Should she?"

"Logically, yes, but life isn't always based on logic." He was about to ask her to dinner when the door opened and in walked Mercy. This time, she was in fitted jeans and a low-cut T-shirt. She was like two sides of a coin. On one side was the sweet schoolteacher, and on the other side was a vixen. She was attractive and intelligent, and she wasn't his type. Apparently, he liked them sassy, and independent, and a challenge. Mercy would never be a challenge.

She completely ignored Natalie standing next to him. "I was heading to Silver Springs and thought I'd invite you to dinner. There's a great chophouse on the outskirts of town. What do you say?"

He wasn't a good liar. In fact, he made it a policy to not lead people on. They'd had tea, and he thought he'd clarified that he wasn't interested, but some people never got it.

"Thanks, Mercy, but I've already got a date." He turned toward Natalie and smiled. "We have to pick Will up from the Mosier's Ranch. I promised him pizza."

Finally, Mercy realized or acknowledged Natalie's presence. "Oh, wow. I didn't know."

Natalie smiled like she did with everyone. It wasn't real because it never reached her eyes. He swore, when it did, the gold flecks sprinkled throughout them sparkled.

"You know he's leaving soon, right?" Natalie set her hand on his arm. "We're mostly friends."

"Yes, I just thought—" Mercy lifted a shoulder in a shrug. "Never mind." She twisted around and headed for the door. "I'll see you around."

When the door closed, he gripped Natalie's shoulders and turned her around to face him. "We're more."

# CHAPTER FIFTEEN

She stood in the middle of Will's room and smiled. "Take that, Fran Dougherty," she said to herself. "You thought I'd fail, but I'm not a quitter." She was bone tired. Splitting her days between the bookstore and the house was wearing on her. Add to that the dinners with Jake, the packing up of her meager belongings, and the endless chatter of Will, she was exhausted. The only thing that seemed to perk her up was Jake's kisses, which were too quick and rarely enough.

The last few days had been busy, between his coaching clients, and her worry over losing her brother. Who would have thought a twelve-year-old kid could bring so much joy into her tiny house? She didn't even mind that he smelled like a dumpster after his days with the Mosiers. Will came with everything from smart-ass comments to dirty socks that stood on their own in the corner, but with all that, he also brought humor and something new. A sense of belonging to something bigger than herself. He brought love. Or at least what she thought love would look like.

"I think it's time to quit for coffee," a deep voice said from the doorway.

She nearly dropped the paintbrush. "Don't sneak up on me like that. I could hurt you."

Jake chuckled. "Are you going to beat me to death with that brush?"

"I could, you know." She turned the wooden handle over and ran her hand from the metal neck to the rounded end. "A little whittling and sanding, and I'd have a shank."

He pushed off the doorway and offered her the cup in his hand. "How about you not shank me and drink this instead?" He turned around in a circle to take in the room. "A splash of cream and one sugar just the way you like it."

She set the brush down and took the coffee he offered.

"I thought you only had beige paint."

"Wes stopped by this morning and brought the blue paint." She lifted her nose into the air and caught the smell of his cologne sitting above the scent of flat latex. When she inhaled again, she breathed in the dark roast coffee.

"Thank you. I don't know why you continue to do nice things for me."

"Because I like you."

She sipped the strong brew, looking over the cup. It was a good thing he was leaving. Too much had happened over the last month that fractured her steely disposition.

"I used to like you, but now that you're my boss, I'm not supposed to. It's bad to crush on your boss."

"I'm not your boss, just the initial financier. You're your own boss."

He moved to the window and was about to lean

on the wall when she reached over and pulled him away. "The paint is wet, and you might ruin that shirt." The blue polo was her favorite. It hugged his body like a glove and was a shade lighter than his eyes.

"Are you worried about me, Keane? Concerned, I might ruin your favorite shirt?"

Her jaw dropped. "How did you ...? I mean, what are you talking about? It's just a shirt."

"You keep lying to yourself. I see how you look at me when I wear this shirt. Why do you think I wear it so often?"

"Because you don't have many clothes. I look at you because I feel sorry you have to wear it three days a week."

He took her cup and set it on the ground before he pulled her into his arms. "I wear it often because it seems to do something for you, and I like affecting you." He nuzzled into her neck.

"Yeah? I'm only affected because you smell bad."

He nibbled at her skin. "Yep, so bad that you walk by me to inhale whenever I'm around."

She tried to push him away, but he held her tighter. "Okay, I may like your cologne."

"Admit it; you like me, I mean ... really like me." He ran his hands up her spine to the back of her head and threaded his fingers through her hair. "I know it in my heart."

"You're lucky to have one of those. Mine stopped beating years ago." Right now, it was beating at twice its rate. The *ka-thump* of its rhythm always sped up around him.

One of his hands moved around to settle between her

breasts. "It's still there; I feel it, beating wildly. And it's telling me that you like me."

As soon as his hand left her chest, she spun out of his arms. "I get the same reaction when I see a spider."

"Okay, we'll go with that for now." He cocked his head to the side. "Where's Will?"

"The guys at the fire station took him today. It was a godsend, really. Can you imagine him being underfoot while I tried to paint? He's a pain in my rear already. I don't need another reason to dislike the little monkey."

Jake laughed. "How is that working for you?"

She bent over to pick up her cup and took a deep drink. "What are you talking about?"

"You might fool yourself into believing you don't like your brother or that you're just doing him a favor. You think you brought him here to save him, but that's the biggest lie. You picked him up and brought him to Aspen Cove to save yourself."

She dropped her cup. The bottom of the Styrofoam container cracked, letting its contents trickle onto the hardwood floor like blood from a pierced heart.

"Are you analyzing me?"

"No, I'm just being honest. Maybe it's time you tried it. You pretend you picked him up because you didn't want him to be in the system, and I think that's partly true, but you also took him in because he's the one person who can't leave you. At least not for six years."

She shook her head. A cross between a squeak and a growl came from her mouth. "You don't know what you're talking about."

"Yep, you're probably right. I've only been mentoring people for years."

"Stop getting into my head." She picked up the now

empty cup and tossed a nearby towel on the spill. "You don't know me. Kissing me doesn't make you an expert."

"You're right. I didn't come here to argue with you. I came here to help."

"You've done enough." Her hand went to her heart.

He shook his head but approached her to lay his hand over hers. "I can feel it beat through your hand. It's okay to feel things, Natalie. Open your heart and let someone in."

"The only thing I'm feeling right now is annoyed because I'm running out of time to get things done." She stepped away and picked up the paint can and brush. "I'll be to work early tomorrow to finish the inventory."

"Finish the house first. The bookstore will be fine."

"I'm not a slacker." She walked into the kitchen to wash the brush.

"No one said you were, but that doesn't mean you can't put yourself first or prioritize."

She squeezed the water from the brush and turned toward him. "A paycheck is a priority."

"It's a guarantee. Now get back to work so you can come to work without a worry." He turned and started for the door.

She followed him. "What? No kiss?"

"I don't kiss people who don't like me."

She moved closer and rested her head on his chest. "But I like your kisses."

"Don't forget my blue shirt and my hugs."

She felt bad that she'd given him a hard time when all he'd done was be kind to her. He'd offered her a full-time, flexible position that paid her more than the diner; more than she'd ever made in her life. No one person had ever done so much for her, so why couldn't she let down her guard with him?

All the stress and changes made her prickly, and that wasn't a good look on her.

"I'm sorry for being a bit—"

He pressed his finger to her lips. "I've met a few bitches in my day, and you're not one. What you are is tired, stressed, and somehow still beautiful."

She wrapped her arms around his waist. Why did hugging him make everything feel okay, if only for a second?

"I'd like to know more about you, Jake. Maybe we can have dinner?"

He leaned back to see her. "Are you asking me on a date?"

She hadn't realized how the question sounded, but it sure resembled a request for a date. Would dating Jake be so bad? Was he right, did she have to let someone in? If so, why couldn't it be him?

She shored her stance and lifted her chin. "I guess I am. Would you like to go on a date with me?"

He bent over and brushed his lips across hers. "You realize there's a certain amount of commitment that comes when you date someone?"

She laughed. "There would be if you weren't temporary, but that's what makes this so great. We'll have fun while you're here."

He opened his mouth to say something. By the look on his face, it was serious. Instead, he took a deep breath and said, "Okay, when do you want this date to be?"

"Did someone say date?" Louise peeked her head through the partially opened door.

"Yep, Natalie here asked me on a date. It would appear she likes my blue shirt and my kisses."

She could feel the heat rise to her cheeks. "I'll like you better when you're gone."

"You'll miss me, and you know it."

She'd never admit to it, but something told her he was right. Everything inside her screamed to not get involved with Jake, but she couldn't help herself. He was the one good thing in all this mess that she would allow herself to have.

"Go away." She gave him a playful shove.

"I'm going. Should I pick you up after I close the bookstore?"

Louise glanced between the two of them. "My goodness, you're really a couple."

"No, we're ..." Natalie shook her head hard enough to rattle her brain. She tried to find the right words to describe them. Friends didn't seem enough, and since she didn't do relationships, anything that sounded more serious wouldn't fit.

"We're a work in progress." He leaned in and gave Natalie a quick peck on the lips. "And she likes my kisses."

"Too cute. When you decide on that date night, bring Will for a sleepover. Brian is a few years younger but put out a bin of action figures, and all boys become ten."

"Perfect, we have a kid sitter. Pick a date, Natalie. You can tell me what it is when I pick you up."

He winked at her before pressing another kiss to her lips. He maneuvered around Louise, who stood in the doorway holding two brown paper sacks.

"Come in," Natalie said.

"I didn't want to interrupt." Louise looked around the

house. "Yep, this is almost identical to the model we have. Only Bobby put an addition in the back once we passed our fifth kid." She lifted the bags. "I brought some things I had in the closet. Curtains and stuff that you might use." She set them on the floor near the wall. "I also wanted to say thank you for giving me your job at the diner. I know you didn't want to leave, but I'm grateful you did."

"Sometimes, you have to sacrifice what you love for what you need. Working at the bookstore will be better for Will and me, and the diner is perfect for you."

"And you and Jake?" Louise lifted a brow. "Don't tell my Bobby, but that man you've got is one giant piece of man-candy."

"He is cute, but he's not mine. He's leaving, so he's a fleeting distraction."

"Mmm mm mm, he doesn't look at you like it's short-lived. He looks at you like you mean something. You can see it in his eyes."

"I promise you it's temporary. He's leaving to partner up with some high-end retreat for the rich and famous."

"We'll see. Last time I saw that look in a man's eyes was over a decade ago. Eight kids later, and Bobby still looks at me like I hung the moon. Hell, on most days, I'm too tired to hang the clothes."

"How did you know Bobby was the one?" She didn't believe in soul mates but liked the stories of how people met.

"There was never anyone else. I loved everything about him from the day I met him. We were high school sweethearts. He's been my first everything. Have you ever been in love?"

Natalie thought back to her high school boyfriend. "I

thought so, and then I let him be my first. Once that was over, he moved on to be a lot of girls' firsts."

Louise wasn't all that much older than Natalie, but she pulled her in for a hug the way a mother would do if she loved her child. "I'm sorry you got a bad apple. It's a good thing there are still good ones out there. Even the bruised ones aren't always bad. Sometimes it takes a little polish and the right recipe. Often they can be sweeter than the day they fell from the tree."

Natalie closed her eyes and thought about the day Doug took her innocence and her heart. She'd run into the house crying to her foster mother about Doug, and all Ellen said was, "I hope you used a condom." There were no words of wisdom or comfort. The reality of the situation was locked down in her heart. Men used women to get what they wanted. Their words of love and forever were emotional currency to buy their way into her pants. That's when she decided she could do the same. Love wasn't something she wanted or needed, but occasionally she liked the feel of a man's arms around her, his kisses on her lips, and his body naked next to hers.

"I'm not looking for forever. I'm still trying to get from one day to the next." She leaned over to take a peek inside the bags. "Thank you for the curtains. They will help to make it appear homier."

"What else do you need?"

She needed everything, but there was no way she'd tell Louise. What little she had could fit in boxes. All the furniture in the tiny house came with the house.

"I'll figure it out. Doc told me to try not to worry about it all at once." She raised her hand to her chest. "That panic attack I had nearly did me in. I'll get the house painted, and I'll figure out how to furnish it later."

By the look of astonishment on Louise's face, she knew she'd said too much.

"You don't have anything?"

"I've got a few things like a frying pan and a few dishes. I was a single woman living alone; I didn't need much."

"What about furniture?"

She didn't want to elaborate, but it opened the can of worms. "It all came with the house. Once I get my car back, I'll hit the secondhand stores and garage sales. I can fit a lot into the back, and what I can't ..."

"Jake can help. Maybe he can borrow Tilden's, Wes's, or Abby's truck. Both of the Bishop boys have them too."

"I'll figure it out." She lifted her thumbnail to her teeth and gnawed on the bit that had grown back. "Everyone has done so many nice things for me ... I just ... I feel bad."

"People help because it makes them feel good too."

"That's what Jake said, but my experiences are different, and in my life, once someone does something nice for me, I seem to owe them. Often the repayment requires far more than the original deed. Far more than I can afford."

Louise waved her hand in the air. "Not here."

Thinking about how much Louise and her family had already given her, she knew she couldn't take anything else. "By the way, I will pay Bobby for his work on my car."

"It's already paid. That man of yours stopped by the diner and handed me a check. I'm not supposed to tell you because he said you wouldn't like it, but I think you need to see how important you are to him."

"I don't know what to say. Thank you."

"Don't thank me, thank Jake. Dress up pretty, and have a beautiful time. I think love is in the air."

"I told you, I'm not looking for love."

Louise turned to walk out. "You know that saying ..."

Natalie didn't have a clue. "What saying?"

"Love isn't something you find. It's something that finds you."

Alone again, she opened the can of paint and started on the living room. "It will never find me if I keep hiding."

# CHAPTER SIXTEEN

He wanted to pull his hair out from the roots. "Natalie, let me buy you some furniture."

"Absolutely not. I can do this on my own."

"Yeah, you can, but you don't have to. Don't let your pride be your biggest mistake."

"You two want to order, or should I give you more time to argue so you can build up a bigger appetite?" Maisey asked.

"We'll order. I'd like a bowl of oatmeal and an endless cup of coffee," Natalie said.

"I'll have a dish of patience and my normal eggs and turkey bacon."

"First lover's quarrel?" Maisey scribbled on the pad and wrote Jake in big letters at the top.

"No, we argue all the time," Natalie said. "He wants to buy me furniture, but he's already fixed my Subaru, given me a job, and so much more."

Maisey winked. "It's the so much more that really counts."

"If I didn't have pride, I'd have nothing."

Jake watched as the two women talked. It had been several days since their last argument, and he was still waiting for the makeup part. With the approaching social worker visit, Natalie was as nervous as a cat in a dog park.

"Sometimes, you have to let your pride go when your need is greater. What do you need?" Maisey asked.

"She needs everything and refuses to accept anything."

Natalie glared at him. "Not true. I took the curtains from Louise. I'm driving my car, and I'm eating the food you bought when we went to Copper Creek."

Maisey sat at the edge of the bench and shoved Natalie over with her hip. "Let me tell you a little story. I was married before Ben. Dalton's father was one mean, miserable cuss. He beat me within an inch of my life multiple times. Then Dalton grew up, and each time he saw his father drinking and getting his mean on, he'd lock him outside and stand guard, so if he got back into the house, he wouldn't get to me. One time he got into the house, and that was when I knew if I didn't leave, Dalton and I would be dead." She glanced around the diner as if to make sure she had enough time to finish. "We lived in my car for a week, and then Doc saved us. He gave me this location and asked me to open a diner. I didn't want to take anything from anyone because that would mean I owed them."

Jake watched Natalie nod her head.

"But you know what? Some people give expecting nothing in return. You're that way, Natalie. I've seen you buy people's meals when they came up short. You gave from your need, not your excess, which means even more. Did you expect them to pay you back?"

Natalie brought her thumbnail to her mouth and

chewed. When there wasn't anything to bite, she dropped her hands into her lap.

"Of course not. I give what I can."

"End of discussion. Let people give what they can. I find, in the worst of times, people are generous. Let Jake be generous." She slid from the booth.

"Maisey," Natalie called out. "Did you ever pay Doc back?"

Maisey laughed. "Nope, I eventually bought the building for about ten cents on the dollar. When I told him that my pride wouldn't allow the handout, he let me make payments, but he never kept the money. He turned around and gave it to others. Calls it his giving fund." She pivoted on her white loafers and walked away.

"Are we fine now? Can we please go into Copper Creek and buy some furniture? I'm pretty sure when Social Services said Will needed a house, it was implied that he'd have a bed to sleep on, and a table to eat his meals."

"Okay, but we shop at the secondhand stores and only get what's necessary." Compromise was the name of the game in life. He had to take his wins where he could. "Should we call Will and ask if he wants to come?"

All the tension released from her shoulders. "I love you for caring about him and wanting to include him in everything." As soon as the words were out, her shoulders tightened, and her eyes moved around like she was looking for an escape.

He reached across the table and took her hand. "Don't worry; I know you weren't telling me you loved me. And I asked about Will coming because I thought you would want to include him. But, when you finally commit to a day for our date, he's not invited."

Once again, she relaxed. "Thank you for everything. I don't know why you do it."

"As I already told you, because I like you."

She smiled. It was genuine and lit up her eyes. "If you tell a soul, I'll deny it, but I like you too. More than I should. More than is safe for my heart."

His heart thundered, somersaulted, and high-fived the lump in his throat. That was a big step for Natalie to admit to liking him. He understood her reluctance to fall completely. He didn't want her to. It would only make it harder to go when he got the call, and he knew he would get the call.

Maisey delivered their drinks and breakfast in one pass.

"Are we calling Will or not?" he asked.

She shook her head. "No, I'm sure he'd rather hang out with Cade and Abby for the day. There are horses and bees, which is so much cooler than beds and tables."

"He's a lucky kid to have you and the people of Aspen Cove."

"Yeah, we're both lucky."

A few days a week, someone came to pick up Will. Luke took him to the fire station. Wes took him to visit the Cooper brothers and the Stevenson Mill. Bobby showed him how to change the oil in his sister's Subaru, which was now working like new. Yesterday, Abby asked to pick him up so he could visit the ranch to ride a horse and visit her hives. For a city kid, he was acclimating to country life well.

"Truth be told, I've been here in Aspen Cove longer than any other place."

"Why is that?" He already knew, but he wasn't sure if she did. Aspen Cove had become the family she craved.

"I don't know. It feels like home."

*Close enough.* "Now that you live in town, I'm sure it will feel more like home. Eat up. I hear furniture shopping can be exhausting."

She took a bite of oatmeal while he ate a piece of his bacon.

"Have you never shopped for furniture?"

He shook his head. "Nope. I had a designer buy everything."

"That's so impersonal."

"At the time, it wasn't important to me."

She sipped her coffee and looked at him as if she were looking inside him. "I bet you live in a sprawling mansion."

"Nope, I live in a townhouse."

She gave him a disbelieving look. "It's the penthouse, right?"

"How did you know?"

"Your work clothes are designer brands, and you have a better manicure than I do." She looked down at her chewed-to-the-nub nails.

"If you'd stop chewing your nails, you could get a manicure. In fact, we could make that a perk of running the bookstore."

She swallowed another bite. "Nope, if I need a manicure, I can get one myself. You already pay me too much."

"Forty thousand a year is hardly too much. You don't know what you're getting yourself into."

"I'll be okay." She scraped the last of her oatmeal from the bottom. "Now that you've hired someone, when will you go?"

"Itching to get rid of me already?"

"No, I just figured ..."

He let out a sigh. "It was a done deal, but I didn't sign the acceptance because I wasn't sure when I'd finish here. I needed a flexible start date at Vision Quest. They took my soft start date as waffling and interviewed a few more candidates."

"Oh no, you gave up your dream to open the bookstore?"

"No, I opened the bookstore because it was important to give back."

She frowned. "See, even you felt like you owed repayment."

He couldn't argue, but it was more than that. "Yes, but not in the way you think. There is absolutely no way to repay someone for the gift of life. I merely wanted to give back. I could have donated a chunk of money to the National Kidney Foundation and been done with it. In fact, I did donate, but this was personal. Once I came here and met Doc, I knew I had to do something special. One of the best gifts a person can give is the gift of knowledge. A bookstore seemed appropriate. Just so happens, Brandy and Bea were avid readers."

"You're amazing."

He laughed. "I am, aren't I?" he teased. "You ready to fill that house with furniture?"

"Only the necessities."

He agreed, but what she didn't take into account was that necessities were subjective. Will would no doubt consider a gaming system and big screen TV a necessity. He always had to have a big chair in the corner with a table and light for reading. It was all perspective.

"NO WAY, THAT'S TOO EXPENSIVE." She ran her hand over the plush upholstery of the sectional sofa that had seen little wear. She pointed to a sagging brown couch that had lived out its life in a frat house. "That one will be better. It's only fifty bucks."

He stepped in front of her and rested his hands on her shoulders. "Let's think long-term here. You buy that couch, and it will need to be replaced by next month. Besides, I'm sure if we took a black light to it, it would glow like Chernobyl with the amount of body fluids embedded into the fabric." He gave her a quick kiss. "Just let me get this one. I like it. You like it, and when I visit, I want to be able to make out with you and not worry about catching anything."

"You're going to visit?"

He thumbed her chin up so he could look into her eyes. "Absolutely. What did you think? That I'd leave and never come back? That I'd abandon you?" He knew that was exactly what she thought because she didn't have any other experience.

"Well, yes."

"Nope, you're stuck with me."

By the lift of her lips, she didn't seem to mind.

"You were supposed to be temporary."

"I'm like a library book you get to check out from time to time."

"I check you out all the time."

How hard was it for her to joke like that with him? Rarely did Natalie let herself go, but he'd seen her protective layers peeling off like onion skin over the last few weeks.

"I know." He touched the buttons of the sage-green

157

polo he wore today. "I think you like this shirt as much as the blue."

"Nope, the blue is still my fave. In fact, I think you should leave it when you go."

"Because you'll miss me?"

Her expression turned serious. "Maybe ... but probably not."

"You're lying to yourself again."

"Yep, but let me live in my lies." She looked past him to the back of the store. "Didn't you say we needed a table?"

"We do." Her use of the word *we* filled him with warmth. Natalie was an I person. She didn't let anyone into her life. Maybe she was referring to Will and her as we, but he had a feeling she included him in the equation.

She immediately went to a table with six chairs and as soon as she saw the price, she moved along. Rather than argue with her on every purchase, he tugged the tag free of the set she liked and shoved it in his pocket.

"This will do."

He smiled and nodded. There was no way he was getting the rickety one just because it was cheap.

"Beds next." He led her to the section of the store with bed frames and mattresses. "No arguments. Just so we're clear, you're not getting a used mattress, and neither is Will for the same reason as the couch."

She frowned. "I'll put a sheet over it."

He shook his head with slow determination. "Nope. When I lay you down on a mattress and make love to you, I don't want to think about how many other people have been there. I want to be the first." *And the only.* Shit, where in the hell did that thought come from? "This is non-negotiable. You can, however, pick out the bedroom sets and dressers, so we know what size mattress to get."

"It's too much."

He narrowed his eyes. "Natalie, consider it a selfish gift. Selfish of me in so many ways. First, there's the sex argument."

"You're confident that I'd let you in my bed."

"I'm hopeful. Then there's the work element. If you have what you need at home, then you'll be happier at work. Now pick out the perfect bedroom set."

"Are you going to commandeer a drawer?"

"Yes, for my blue shirt. Let's get this done so they can deliver today."

She huffed. "That will cost a fortune."

"Think of all the money you saved me by shopping at a consignment store."

She moved down the aisles of the bedroom sets. "I've never had my own set. I can't remember ever having a dresser."

"What do you use now?"

"Will and I have plastic bins."

"Not good enough." He moved to a simple shaker style bed made from solid hardwood. He knew it would be pricey, but it would last. "Do you like this one?"

She reached for the tag, but he stopped her from seeing it.

"Do you like it, or is there another one of equal quality that you like better?"

"I love it."

He yanked the tag free and shoved it into his pocket.

"Let's get something awesome for Will." He led her down the aisle.

They found a bunk bed set that had a full-sized bed

on the bottom and a twin on top for sleepovers. When he outgrew the bunk bed part, they could dismantle it and leave the full-sized bed intact. It was the perfect bed for a growing boy. Jake pulled the tag, and they made their way to the front.

"Ring these up and put them on this card," he told the owner. "I'll pay what's necessary to have them delivered today."

Natalie fidgeted next to him. He knew it was overwhelming for her.

"My crew can be there at two." The owner handed him his card and the receipt, which he shoved into his pocket before she could see it.

"Perfect. That gives us time to hit Costco again for more essentials."

"What else could I need?"

"Oh sweetheart, there's so much I could give you." His comment was filled with innuendo.

"You're way too much."

He laughed. "I've been told."

She slugged him in the arm as they walked out.

Two hours later, they parked in front of the house only to find bags and boxes of stuff on the porch.

"What the hell?" Natalie asked. "What did you do?"

"Nothing. Looks like you got bags of love."

She burst into tears, and he pulled her into his arms. "I don't deserve any of this. I'm so unworthy."

"Hey," he scolded. "You are worthy of this and more. Remember, love can't enter a locked door. Open yourself up to it, and you'd be surprised at how worthy a recipient you'll become."

"I don't know how to love." She hiccupped between sobs. "I've never been loved."

"Not true. You're loved by everyone in town. While you don't think you deserve love, everyone else can see that you do. Look at what you did for Will."

"I didn't love him. I didn't know him."

"You loved him enough as a human to save him. That's love, Natalie. Bask in it."

She opened the door, and they entered the house. "Thank you for always knowing what to say."

He grinned. "I'd like to say it's my job, but with you" —he tapped his chest—"it comes from my heart and not my head." He kissed her long and deep, hoping to show her how worthy of being loved she was. If he didn't keep things in check, he'd be head over heels in love with her already, but he was leaving, and that kind of love wouldn't serve either of them well. He'd convinced himself that what he felt for her was the same love he felt for humanity. That was his lie.

"It's like Christmas out there."

"Shall we bring in the presents and open them?"

# CHAPTER SEVENTEEN

Natalie rearranged the throw pillows on the couch again. They were part of the bounty left on the porch, along with a crocheted throw.

"You okay?"

She walked to the window and peeked behind the curtains. "No." She looked down the hallway to where Will's door sat open. From where she stood, she could see him lying on his bed reading the newest Harry Potter book Jake had brought him. "What if they take him?"

He walked to where she paced the floor in front of the window. "They won't take him." He opened his arms, and she gladly fell into them.

Jake had been her rock. He'd spent every night that week helping her make the house into a home. She couldn't believe it was the same place.

"How do you know?"

"Why would they remove him from his family who loves him and cares for him?"

"Love?" She shook her head. "It's not about that."

"Don't fool yourself. Look at what you've done here."

She glanced around the house. It was straight out of a shabby chic magazine. Maybe shabbier than chic, but it felt like a home.

"You can give the kid a home, but a home without love is not a home." He hugged her tighter to his chest. "This sure feels like a home. If you didn't care for him, you wouldn't worry that they'd take him. He used to live with a crack dealing father who had a line of prostitutes out the door waiting to provide whatever service they could for their next fix. Do you think he felt loved there?"

"He told you that?" It shocked her that they'd shared so much.

"He told us both about the crack ho, but he's been opening up to me, and I can tell you that being here is far better than anywhere he's lived. And having heard his story, I'm shocked he's as stable as he is. That's a testament to his strength."

She smiled. "I guess we got something good from our dad. Maybe a backbone of steel."

"Are you going to pace the floor like a caged animal, or kiss me?"

She rubbed her face. "I'm going to kiss you." She glanced at the old clock sitting on the mantel. Peter Larkin had brought it over yesterday. He told her to put it somewhere she could see it to remind her that time passes too quickly. She thought it was a sweet gesture until he told her she could also use it to time her man's stamina. "Will you stay with me for a while longer?"

He tilted her chin. "I'm not leaving you. I'll stay with you forever."

Those words hugged her heart. She knew he meant

he'd stay for now and not a lifetime, but she let herself dream for a moment about a life together. A life where they lived in this house and walked to the bookstore hand in hand each morning. He could take his coaching calls in the office while she manned the counter. Once school started, Will could get off the bus and come straight to the Book Nook to do his homework and bury himself into the corner bean bag he loved.

On Wednesdays, he'd do his Winding Down with Will event, and the kids from the town would gather in the corner to listen to him read.

"What brought that smile to your face?"

She hadn't realized she was smiling. "Just thinking about the future. It's not wise to plan too far ahead, but sometimes I let myself."

He brushed his lips across hers. "It's okay to dream."

"That's all it is—a dream." She moved over to the couch and plopped down, messing up the perfectly aligned pillows. "Tell me about your dreams."

He took the seat beside her. "They've changed over the years. A brush with death can do that to a person."

"I'm sure, but most people who have a close call don't work harder, they usually think about family and stuff like that."

He settled in and tugged her to his side. "Jenny left me when she found out I had a life-threatening disease. She said she couldn't invest the time to build a relationship only to have me die on her."

She sat up to look at him. That old hurt still lingered in his eyes. "You're shitting me."

"Nope, she left the week after my diagnosis, and I never saw her again." He chuckled. "I got a postcard from her five years later. She was on her honeymoon and said she was thinking of me and hoped I was doing well."

"Awful. That's why I don't let myself get too attached." She leaned into him, resting her head on his shoulder. She breathed him in. When he left, that was one thing she'd miss. The smell of him always calmed her.

"Getting attached isn't the problem. Getting hurt is the issue. Be wise in your choices, and you might end up okay. I didn't choose wisely."

"That's why you don't choose. Not letting someone into your heart is safer." She placed her hand over his chest. "That's what makes us a perfect fit. Neither one of us expects anything more than what we've got at the moment."

"You're too young to be so cynical."

She made a motorboating sound with her lips. "I'm only six years younger than you, but I feel a million years older."

"You've been through a lot. I imagine at six you were already thirty in your soul." He kissed the top of her head. "What about you? Have you ever been in love?"

"Once, or so I thought." She breathed in and exhaled. "There was a high school boy who wooed me until I gave him my virginity, then he wooed the next stupid girl. I think he had a jar where he collected the tears of all the girls he deflowered."

"Shit. I'm sorry. Don't let one asshole ruin love for you."

"It was a long time ago. I'm not pining for him. It is what it is. If you ask me, love is overrated. I think it's a feeling that starts in your sex organs and inhibits the flow of oxygen to the brain."

"Not true; love can be amazing when it's with the right person."

The squeak of brakes had her bolting from the couch to look out the window. "Oh my God, she's here." Feeling light-headed, she bent over so the blood could rush to her head.

"Do you want me to stay?"

"Yes ... no ... I don't know. What's better?"

"I'll stay."

A knock sounded at the door. She moved toward it, taking several deep breaths. She dried her sweaty palms on her slacks and pasted on her well-practiced smile before she opened the door and stepped aside.

"Welcome to our home." It was weird to say those words. She'd lived many places, but none had ever felt like home. She glanced around at the furnishings. The townsfolk had set her up nicely with everything from dishes to bar soap, but it wasn't the things in the house that made it feel homey, it was the people. The solid presence that others brought with it. That was something she couldn't buy.

"Good afternoon, Natalie. Thank you for sending me your new address." She glanced over her shoulder at the yard. It was mostly mowed weeds, but that was next on her list. Sheriff Cooper had visited two days ago and told her he'd help her on the weekend. Apparently, he loved to garden and was happy to volunteer his rake and hoe.

"We are working on the house a little at a time. I've had a lot of help from the community. The yard is next."

Fran Dougherty walked inside with a clipboard in her hand. "I'm surprised at the progress you've made."

She didn't know how to take that. Had she expected her to fail? "I can do anything once I put my mind to it."

Fran scratched some notes on her clipboard and looked up. Her smile broadened when she noticed Jake.

"And who might this be?"

He moved in to offer his hand for a shake. "I'm Jake Powers, a friend of Natalie's."

She hadn't had many friends in her life, and deep inside, she knew Jake was one. He'd been there for her when many would have bailed. He'd held her while she cried. Wiped her tears away and kissed her until her insides glowed with happiness. Yes, Jake was definitely a friend.

"You're not *that* Jake Powers, are you?" Fran pulled her phone out and queued his book up on her Kindle App. "I love this book." She turned the screen to Natalie. "Have you read *Love the Life You Live*?"

She shook her head. "I don't have to read his words; he's here every day to dole out his wit and wisdom."

"Lucky girl." She smiled back at Jake. "You're far more handsome in person."

Natalie stepped back to watch the exchange, and jealousy burned at her insides. She had no real claim to Jake, but while he was in Aspen Cove, she considered him to be hers.

"You're too kind." He moved beside Natalie and wrapped his arm around her shoulder. "Did you want a tour of the house, or would you prefer to go about it on your own? I was about to make tea. I can make it for three if you'd like."

Natalie wanted to kick his shin. Tea would only extend the visit, and what she wanted was Fran Dougherty to fill out her report and be gone.

"I'd love tea." Fran glanced at Natalie after a long stare at Jake. "Shall we?"

"Absolutely." She twirled around. "This is the living room." She brushed by Jake and went to the kitchen. It still had harvest-gold appliances, but with the addition of eyelet curtains and a sunflower picture hanging above the kitchen table, it looked purposeful—like the color scheme was supposed to be retro 70s. "And the kitchen."

Fran pointed to the refrigerator. "May I?"

"Of course." She wasn't worried this time around. Another trip to Copper Creek with Jake had filled her cupboards and refrigerator full of everything from block cheese to spinach.

Jake brushed past her. "I'll get the tea ready." He leaned in and whispered, "Relax."

"That one's a keeper," Fran said. "A man who makes tea is a good find."

"Oh, I'm not keeping him. He's only in town for a bit."

Fran frowned. "Too bad. I bet he's been a good influence on Will." She jotted more notes on the page attached to her clipboard. "Is Will home?"

"He's in his room reading."

Fran's eyes opened wide. "By choice, or is he in trouble?"

Natalie laughed. "I think he found his love of reading because he got sent to his room while his father ... I mean, our father did business. But he's reading by choice. Now that I'm managing the bookstore in town, he has lots of opportunities to exercise his passion." She told Fran about his reading nook for the kids, and how the town had embraced having him. "He spends one afternoon a week at the fire station, and one day a week on a ranch outside of town where he's learning about horses and bees."

"Interesting."

They walked into Will's room.

"Hey Will, how's it going?"

He stuck a bookmark inside to keep his page and set the book on his comforter. "It's awesome. Do you see my room?"

She walked around the space. "It's a great room."

It was Natalie's favorite space with its blue walls and red accents. The bunk bed took up half the room, and the dresser and desk took up the other half. On the walls, Will had taped pictures he'd drawn of the things he loved about Aspen Cove, like Cade's horse Sable, and Bowie Bishop's boat dock that Will had visited last week. He'd even drawn a stick figure of her. Albeit, the resemblance was not good except for her smile, which she seemed to do a lot more lately.

"Who's the dog?" Fran pointed to the rough sketch of Otis, Sage and Cannon's dog, who had three legs.

"That's Otis. He's a tripod, but he doesn't know it. His best friend is Bishop, who still has puppy brains. Sometimes Clovis is around, but he's fat and waddles from place to place until his owner Trig picks him up." Will's eyes grew bright. "Trig is missing a leg below his knee. He's a war hero, and he has twin boys. They're still babies, though, so they aren't much fun."

"Sounds like you're fitting in around here."

He lifted his shoulders in a shrug. "Sure. Everyone is nice." He frowned. "Everyone but Dr. Lydia. I mean, she's nice, but she likes to give shots."

Fran turned to Natalie. "You have his immunizations complete? What about registering for school?"

"I called the school, but we have to wait until August to register. He's also scheduled next month for the dentist." There wasn't one in town, but Copper Creek had plenty of them to choose from.

Fran made a few more notes and turned back toward the hallway. She did a cursory check of the remaining rooms and headed straight for Jake and tea.

"Everything good?" Jake asked. He'd set the table for four. On a plate, in the center, he'd placed the muffins Katie had brought by, and the honey Abby sent over with Will.

"I think so." Natalie looked at Fran with a hopeful expression. "Is everything okay?"

Fran took a seat and doctored her tea with a hefty serving of honey. "You've done everything I asked for and more. You must really love your brother."

She'd never admit to that, but she liked him. He reminded her of herself when she was younger. "He's a good kid, and I wanted to give him a chance to have a good life."

Jake reached over and set his hand on Natalie's. "He's growing on her. Natalie might not admit to loving him, but she does."

"Well, you know the saying ... you can't experience love until you love someone more than yourself."

"I was recently told"—she looked at Jake with what she hoped was affection—"that you have to love yourself to love another."

Will walked in. "Do I have to drink tea?" It was a half whine because, despite his complaints, Will liked tea.

"I made you some hot cocoa, bud. Your cup is on the counter. Microwave for thirty seconds, and don't burn yourself."

"Too bad you're not staying, Jake, because you make a good-looking little family."

At the mention of family, she asked Fran, "Does that mean Will can stay?"

Fran's head began to nod before the affirmation came out. "Yes, but I'll be back. A few weeks doesn't represent a lifetime, but I like what I see." She finished her tea and pushed her cup forward. "Do you want to stay with your sister, Will?"

Will took the empty seat next to Jake. "Yes, ma'am. She's the only family I have, and I love her."

A lump stuck in her throat. All eyes turned to her. She opened her mouth, but nothing came out. Looking at Will, she could see he needed to hear the words too. She forced the ball of emotion down with a swallow.

"I love you too, Will."

They stared at each other for about ten seconds. It was the longest ten seconds of her life, but also some of the best. She had a family and telling her brother she loved him, didn't end with the earth swallowing her up. Her eyes went to Jake. What about him? She felt the same way, but with Jake, was it love or gratitude? She couldn't be certain.

"I've got to go." Fran slid her chair out. "Best visit I've had all week. Thank you for that." She walked over to Will, who had a chocolate mustache. "You take care of your sister, too."

"Yes, ma'am. I will."

They walked the social worker to the door, and when she left, Will threw himself into both of their arms. The three of them stood behind the closed front door and hugged until Jake's phone buzzed with an incoming message.

He stepped back, pulled his phone from his pocket, and smiled. "Hey Will, would you mind if I took your sister on a real date? Louise has asked you to spend the night. Eric and Brian are dying to play with you."

"You want to take me on a date?" Natalie asked.

"You were supposed to take me, but if I waited for you to pick one, I'd be too old to walk. You said as soon as everything settled down. Looks like things are settled."

"Do you think they have cooler Legos than we have at the bookstore?" Will asked.

"I don't know, but you can see. If you don't want to sleep over, then you can come to dinner with us. It is a celebration."

Will's nose scrunched up. "Yuck, I'll definitely pass. I don't want to have to watch the way you look all googly-eyed at each other." He frowned. "Just don't do it on my bed, okay?"

"What?" Natalie asked. "We won't do it anywhere." She risked a glance at Jake, but his expression said otherwise. A bolt of heat pulsed through her.

"Louise will pick him up after her shift, and I'll pick you up at six." He ruffled Will's hair. "Clean your face, and pack a bag."

Will took off down the hallway.

"Are you going to order me around too?" She wasn't offended that he took on a parental role with Will because her brother seemed to thrive around Jake. She liked the strength of a man who could step in and take charge.

He leaned in and kissed her like he owned her, and for a minute, she'd let him.

"Yes, put on your prettiest dress." He whispered, "I'd love to try out that mattress tonight if you're game."

Her skin prickled with excitement. "You know me and still want me?"

"Since the day you tried to kill me with salt." He let

his hands slide down her body to grip her bottom. "Who wouldn't want you?"

"Pretty much everyone."

His hands moved up to capture her cheeks. "Isn't it time someone became everything you didn't know you were looking for?"

# CHAPTER EIGHTEEN

He couldn't decide on the flowers, so he bought them all. The front seat of his SUV had everything from roses to hydrangeas. On the floorboard were two boxes of chocolates.

"It's just a date," he told himself. He parked and sat for a moment. He hadn't dated in a decade. He'd had plenty of sex. Hookups required nothing but his presence. Somehow, this was different. Maybe because he'd gotten to know Natalie, and he really liked her.

He gathered the flowers and made his way to the door. She opened it before he got there. Standing before him was a beautiful woman dressed in a bold emerald-green dress and nude heels. Her hair hung in soft waves over her shoulders.

"Did someone die?" She stood back and gave him room to enter.

"I did, just now, when you opened the door. You're stunning." He looked at the dozens of flowers in his hands. "These are dull compared to you."

"Seriously, did you rob a funeral home? I've never

seen so many flowers." She led him into the kitchen, where he emptied his hands of the blooms.

"I couldn't decide. The roses reminded me of your lips. The sunflowers of how you stand tall despite adversity. The hydrangeas are soft and delicate but can withstand harsher elements. The daisies are bright and happy, like your smile. The stargazer lilies smell almost as sweet as you do. You needed them all, so I got them all."

"Where am I supposed to put them? I don't own a vase. No one has ever bought me flowers."

He held a finger in the air and walked out the kitchen door to the back patio where the mop bucket sat. "Will this do for now?"

"It's perfect."

He filled the bucket with water and helped her arrange the flowers inside the gray plastic container.

"Did Louise pick up Will?"

"Yes, and he was so excited, but he reminded me that his room was off-limits."

"He knows way too much for being so young." He set his hands on her shoulders. "We don't need his room. We've got yours."

"Do you think buying out the flower store is a sure way to get into my pants?"

He slid his hands down her arms and moved to rest them on the curve of her hips. "You're not wearing pants. And if I get my way tonight, you won't be wearing this despite how beautiful you look in it." He gave her a quick peck on the lips and walked her to the door.

When he helped her into the SUV, she saw the boxes of candy on the floorboard. "Are these to sweeten me up in case the flowers didn't work?"

"No, I didn't have enough hands to grab everything. Those are because you deserve sweetness in your life."

"You sure pull out all the stops for a girl."

"I've got candles, too, just in case."

"A planner. That sounds about right. A man like you doesn't get where he wants to be without preparation."

"Don't forget the kidney disease."

She buckled in while he rounded the car to get into the driver's seat.

He started the engine and headed toward Copper Creek.

"That really bothers me that Jenny left you. You were in love with her, and she abandoned you when you needed her the most."

"I understand why. Hell, I would have abandoned me too. It wasn't pretty. She thought I'd die."

"We all die. It takes one step in front of a moving car, a fall, or a moment of despair. All we have is this minute. This second is the only future we're guaranteed."

"That's poetic coming from someone who doesn't believe in love."

"All I'm saying is you can't get caught up in the future. Carpe Diem."

"That's right, seize the day."

Thirty minutes later, they pulled into Trevi's Steakhouse. "I've never been here." She moved her thumb to her teeth. "I would have been good with pizza and burgers too."

"Stop chewing your nails. This is a celebration. You changed a kid's life in a month. That deserves something nice."

"I had a lot of help. I don't want to owe—"

He leaned over and covered her mouth with his.

176

When he was certain he'd kissed the words from her lips, he moved back. "Stop thinking you owe anyone. I'm not taking you to a nice place because I expect a payback." The valet stood at his door, but Jake raised a hand, signaling he needed one more minute. "I hope that when we get back to your place, I can seduce you, but that has nothing to do with money or gifts or gratitude. My desire comes from being a man who sees what he likes—who likes what he sees—a man who'd love to see a lot more." He turned to the window and nodded, and the valet opened the door then rushed around to open Natalie's.

"Thank you for everything."

"You're welcome." He led her into the restaurant where a table was waiting. The view was spectacular with the sun setting behind the mountain, and the sky was a blend of purple and orange.

The waitress arrived. She barely registered that he was there with Natalie. Her flirting was over the top.

"You look like a scotch man. How about a two-finger plunge?" Her voice was husky and wanton. He considered her offer both inappropriate and rude.

He reached for Natalie's hand and held it. "My wife and I would like a bottle of Penfold's and a new server, please."

It was as if she'd just noticed Natalie. In his mind, Natalie was someone a person couldn't miss.

The waitress left in a huff.

"Your wife?" She didn't let go of his hand. In fact, her fingers threaded through them as if she was also claiming him.

"It stops that rude behavior right away."

"Do you experience that a lot? Where a woman only sees you in a room?"

"No, but I only see you."

The manager came over, and after Jake explained the total disregard and lack of respect for his "wife," the manager offered the pricy bottle of wine as an apology.

They spent the next hours sipping a fabulous cabernet and eating. Natalie had the filet while he opted for the salmon. He loved listening to her talk, especially if he could get her to talk about herself. She'd been through a lot in her life, from the abandonment of one parent to the death of another, and yet she pushed on. She wasn't a Pollyanna, but she wasn't bitter either. To her, life was a crapshoot, and she dealt with the blows it gave her.

On the ride back home, she asked, "When will you be leaving?"

It had been over a week since his last conversation with Matt Steinman. At any other time, he would have been unhappy with the developments. Not that the delay pleased him, but it gave him more time to get to know Will and Natalie—more time to make sure the bookstore would be in good hands.

"I don't know. I haven't heard from the owner of Vision Quest. Are you trying to get rid of me?"

She lowered her head. "No, I'm wondering if tonight will be a one-time event or ..." He couldn't see the color of her cheeks in the darkness, but he was certain they'd be pink.

"Let's see how it goes. I could be awful in bed."

She laughed. "If you"—she cleared her throat—"have sex like you kiss, then I'm sure you'll ruin me for all other men."

"Now, you're stroking my ego."

She leaned over and whispered. "If you're lucky, maybe something else."

He hit the gas and got home in twenty-five minutes versus the thirty it would normally take. While he was happy to push the speed limit a little, there was no sense in being careless.

He opened her door. She hugged the boxes of candy all the way inside. "I'll check on Will to make sure he's good."

He kissed her. "I'll do my thing then."

"What is your thing?"

"Today, it's pleasing you." While Natalie called about Will, he picked a few roses from the bucket in the kitchen and took a detour to the back of the SUV for the candles.

He went to work plucking petals from the red roses and laying them in a heart pattern on the bed. He lit the candle and walked into the living room where she sat on the sofa, chewing her nail.

"What's wrong?"

"I'm nervous. It's been a long time, and maybe you won't like me after." The words spilled out quickly. "I value your friendship and might ruin it if I'm bad in bed."

He held out his hand. "Come here. There's no way you're bad in bed. And you don't have to do anything you don't want to do. I'll still be your friend if you say no."

"But I want to. I desperately want to."

He tugged her to his chest. "Would it help if I told you I was nervous too?"

"No, one of us has to know what they're doing."

He chuckled. "Then, I won't tell you. Let's go." He led her to the bedroom where the candle flickered, casting dancing shadows on the newly painted walls.

"You made a heart of petals."

"Do you like it?"

She turned around, and he saw the firelight glint off

her tears. "Yep, I'm ruined. Tonight will go down in history as the most romantic night of my life."

He hated that she hadn't been treated well before, but he vowed to treat her right while he was there.

"You can still say no."

"Yes." She reached behind her to unzip her dress.

"Nope. I've been dreaming about taking this dress off you all night." He turned her around and pressed kisses along her neck until goose bumps rose from her skin. Slowly, one tooth at a time, he unzipped the emerald dress. It slipped from her shoulders and fell to the floor in a puddle at her feet.

She hid her curves under ill-fitting jeans and loose T-shirts, but Natalie was a goddess with ample breasts and a narrow waist that curved out at her hips. Hips that could hold a man and rock him for hours.

"Beautiful."

She wasn't wearing lace undergarments. Hers were sturdy cotton, but they looked as sexy as any satin or lace getup he'd ever seen. She turned around and started on the buttons of his shirt, kissing his chest with each one she got loose. When the last one was freed, he shrugged his shirt off and let it fall to the floor beside her dress.

Her fingertips danced over his skin, stopping at the scar on his side. It was a massive line that curved into what looked like a C. It had mostly faded to silvery-white, but there were a few pink spots. She dropped to her knees and pressed her mouth to those places that hadn't healed well.

"This is beautiful." Her tongue ran along the raised scar until she was back on her feet before him. "This scar is the reason you're standing before me now."

He couldn't believe this woman thought his disfigurement was a beautiful affirmation of life. He'd always thought so too, but many women pretended it didn't exist.

"I'm tired of standing." He walked her back until the back of her knees hit the mattress, and she fell into the petals in slow motion. Her shoes hit the floor at the same time he kicked off his. "Are you sure, Natalie? This takes our friendship to a whole new level."

She lifted and tugged at the button of his pants. In a matter of seconds, they were gone, along with his boxer briefs. He was naked, and she was still wearing white cotton underwear.

Sliding onto the bed, he pulled her next to him. "You make me feel things I haven't felt in forever." With her hand in his, he moved her fingers to his lips.

She thrust her hips forward until his length pressed to her stomach. "I feel it too." She giggled.

Her breath went from calm to panting with every kiss and languid stroke. He peeled the straps of her bra down and suckled her rose-colored buds until she squirmed beside him.

"More," she breathed into a kiss. "I need more."

This wasn't a woman who forgot how to make love. Natalie was filled with passion and need. He removed the rest of her clothing and explored her body with his tongue. Each time he felt her tense and moan, he pulled back.

"You're torturing me."

"No." He shook his head. "I'm worshipping you." A rose petal stuck to her hip. He picked it up and skimmed it over her sensitive flesh.

When all he heard was a litany of please, please, please, he reached for the condom he'd put on the night-stand and rolled it on his length. Braced on his hands above her, he stared into her eyes. Eyes filled with so many questions he couldn't answer. What was this thing between them? Where would it take them? Was it wise?

With a single steady press, he buried himself inside her.

"Are you with me?" he asked.

"I feel so close that I am you."

He thrust and retreated at a steady pace. Her hands roamed his body while he took in the soft sensation of being inside her. The heat moved through him until it settled inside his heart. Full to bursting with emotion, he blurted, "I could love you."

She gripped his hips and pulled him in as deep as he could go. "Then love me while you're here."

Her words ignited a fire in him. Natalie was open to his love—at least temporarily.

"I'll love you forever." Words said in the throes of passion were easy to ignore after the fact, but he knew his were true. He would love Natalie on some level for the rest of his life. "Look at me." He picked up his pace and increased his depth until they were shaking from the need to release. Her body tensed, and her core fluttered, but it was his name leaving her lips in a moan that had him following her into bliss. And when the final shudder left him, and he rolled to his side, pulling her with him, he knew everything had changed.

# CHAPTER NINETEEN

She rolled over and pressed her nose to his chest. She used to think pheromones were fiction, but Jake had a scent that spoke to her soul.

"Did last night really happen?" Every muscle in her body ached with delicious memories of their lovemaking. At least that's what she'd call it in her head. It felt exactly what she imagined love would be like if love were possible for her.

Having sex with a one-night stand didn't require emotions, but she'd run the gamut of them with Jake. Everything from elation to fear.

"If it didn't, I hope I fall back to sleep and dream it again." He rubbed his hand along her back in a lazy, comfortable fashion—like he'd been doing it for years. "Do you want coffee?"

"I can get it." She attempted to roll away, but he held her in place.

"Let me get it. You stay in bed. Isn't it time someone waited on you?"

She giggled. "I like the sound of that."

He rolled from the bed. Seeing the firm globes of his backside was a morning bonus of getting up after him. He tugged on his pants and found his shirt in the pile of clothes hastily discarded last night.

"I'll be back."

She rolled to her back and smiled. Was it possible to be this happy? She knew it wasn't a forever thing. Life was fluid, and the best way to survive it was to ride the ebb and flow.

Weeks ago, if anyone said she'd be living in a house, working in a job that paid regularly, and spending the night with a man who could be considered a god of passion, she wouldn't have believed it. Add in Will, who was unexpected but not unwanted, and her life was nearly perfect. Nearly; because this wasn't real. The house was on loan, Jake was temporary, and Will was still in the honeymoon phase. She had to get through his teens, which were tough on everyone. Those were worries for another day. Today she'd bask in the glory of a perfect night with a perfect man.

The smell of coffee drifted through the air. As she closed her eyes and inhaled, a loud banging came from the front room.

She bolted from the mattress and pulled on the robe she had hanging from a hook behind the door.

"Let me in," Will screamed from the other side.

She tied the waist while rushing to answer. With his shirt unbuttoned and his hair just out of bed messy, Jake met her there. There wasn't time to hide the fact that they'd just gotten out of bed. Instead, she pulled it open to reveal her little brother, who had tears running down his face.

He rushed past her and into his room, slamming the door.

Louise stood on the porch wearing a frown. "I'm so sorry." She glanced at Jake and then her. "Looks like I might have ruined the moment."

Natalie knew what it looked like. It appeared exactly as it was. She and Jake had been in bed.

"What happened?" Her heart thumped inside her chest. A hundred garbled thoughts went through her head. "Did he do something wrong?"

Louise shrugged. "No, it was a kid fight. They were playing with action figures, and one went missing. Brian accused Will of taking it, and he took it to heart."

She and Jake said, "Oh," at the same time.

"Do you think he took it?" Jake asked.

"No, but it is missing, and until it shows up, Brian will be convinced he did."

"Do you want to come in?" Natalie felt bad that she hadn't offered before. She wasn't particularly social and hadn't considered what might be appropriate.

"No, I've got to run." She reached out a hand and laid it on Natalie's arm. "Will is a good kid. I loved having him and want to have him over again. Hopefully, this blows over quickly with the boys." She glanced at Jake, who was buttoning up his shirt. "Glad you guys had a good time."

The heat of a blush crept up her cheeks. "We did, and thank you." She felt like she owed Louise an answer to Will's behavior, but saying he used to be a thief would only make him look guilty. "Will is adjusting to a lot. His reputation as a new kid in town is important. If the toy doesn't show up, let us know."

Louise laughed. "Oh, honey, with eight kids around, Will stealing it is the last consideration. Most likely, Jill flushed it down the toilet, but I'll let you know. Tell Will I'm sorry on behalf of Brian."

Louise left, and they closed the door.

"How should I handle this?" Natalie asked. She was completely out of her element. She'd never been a parent and hadn't had good role models.

"Are you talking about the potential theft or him coming home to us being half-dressed and together?"

"Oh, hell, I hadn't even thought of that." She rubbed her face and dropped her hands. "Let's take the bull by the horns. No use dancing around both subjects." She turned toward the hallway and called out, "Will, come here, please."

"I'll get the coffee," Jake said.

Will dragged his feet toward the living room. When he was a few feet away, he lunged toward Natalie, and buried his head in her chest and cried.

She took him to the couch and sat, where he spent the next few minutes shedding tears.

Jake came in with one cup of coffee and two cups of cocoa. "Hey, let's talk."

Will sat back and swiped the tears with the back of his hand. It broke her heart because for Will to cry, it must have wounded him greatly.

"They accused me of stealing."

Natalie looked at Jake, hoping he'd step in, but she knew he wouldn't. Not because he didn't want to, but because he respected her authority. That was one thing she loved about him. He could have run roughshod over her with his money and influence, and yet, he never did. He understood that she needed to be independent—until it came to mattresses. That was the only time he ignored her wishes, and deep inside, she was glad. It was the first new thing she'd had, and the memory of making love to him for the first time would always remain tucked in the fibers.

"Did you take it?" she asked.

"No," he wailed. "I'm not a thief anymore."

"Okay then. Did you help look for it?"

"No, why would I?"

"Because it's the right thing to do. If you had helped look for it, then you'd appear less guilty. Instead, you grabbed your bag and came home."

She could see the cogs of his brain turning. If Will was like her, he was emotionally stunted, which came from poor parenting. If no one explained right from wrong and good from bad, there wasn't a gauge to use when faced with these types of situations. She'd learned from years of mistakes and lots of trials and errors.

"Aren't you innocent until proven guilty?" he asked.

Jake sat back like a psychologist observing an intervention. He didn't say a word.

"That's what it's supposed to be, but public opinion weighs heavily, and while the premise of innocence is a good one, it's not accurate. Once accused, it falls on you to prove your innocence."

"I offered to show them my backpack. Do you want to see it?"

"No." She laid a comforting hand on his shoulder. "I believe you."

His eyes opened wide. "You do?"

"I do." She looked at Jake and said, "Do you have anything to add?"

He rubbed his scruffy chin, and she shivered at the memory of his facial hair tickling the inside of her thighs.

"Did you feel guilty when Brian blamed you?"

She cocked her head. "If he wasn't guilty, why would he feel guilty?"

It didn't take Will a second thought to answer. "I did. I even thought maybe I'd taken it in my sleep."

Jake chuckled.

It didn't seem like a laughing matter, but it intrigued her with where this was going. She tugged her robe tighter, grabbed her coffee, and sat back to watch the master at work.

"That's your subconscious reminding you of the mistakes you got away with. You know that you've stolen things before, and the guilt is an automatic response because you're a good person, Will. As time goes by, you'll have more confidence, and your good behavior will outshine your bad behavior. When another situation like this comes up, your brain will say, 'impossible because I'd never do that' and that will be the truth."

Will thought for a few seconds. "Is my brain broken?"

"Not at all. It's working perfectly. Your internal compass is guiding you on a good path."

"What if they never find it? I liked playing with Brian. He's the only kid close to my age in town."

"I'm sure it will be all right."

Will looked at Jake. "Can I hug you, or is that weird for guys?"

Jake pulled Will in for a big hug. "Not weird at all. We may be men"—he puffed out his chest—"but we're still human, and all humans need connection."

Will sat back. "Can I ask you something else?"

Jake shrugged. "Sure."

"Did you spend the night with my sister?"

Jake swallowed hard and stared at her for the save.

She smiled and gave him a look that said, "I'll handle it."

"I don't want to lie to you, Will. If I told you no, he didn't, that wouldn't be honest. Even if I lied, you wouldn't believe me because you're too smart and wise for your years. Yes, Jake and I had a date, and he spent the night. Does that bother you? Do you have appropriate questions?" She added appropriate because Will might ask anything, and she didn't have the energy to explain the mechanics of sex to a twelve-year-old.

Will looked between them, and his lips upturned into a grin. "Yes, it's okay, and no, I don't have questions. I know all about the birds and the bees." He turned to Jake and high-fived him. "We may be men, but men need a connection too."

All three burst into laughter that stopped when the doorbell rang.

Will bounded off the couch to answer it. Standing on the porch was Brian Williams. His hands were in his pockets, and his head was hung low.

His father, Bobby, stood behind him. "Go on, now. Tell him."

Brian rocked from side to side. "I'm sorry. I found my action figure in my sisters' room. They decided Barbie needed a new boyfriend." He shook his head. "Can we be friends?"

She and Jake walked behind Will and watched for his reaction. He took a deep breath. "Sure. I'm sorry I didn't help find him."

"I don't blame you. The last time I walked into the girls' room, they tried to give me a makeover." Brian pushed his hand forward for a shake. "Truce?"

Will reached out, but only got halfway. "Next time, remember that people are innocent until proven guilty."

The boys shook hands.

Bobby patted his son's back. "Let's go home. Your mom wants your room cleaned before she gets home from her shift."

Brian groaned. "Dang it. I thought Will could come over and play."

"Let's ask your mom when she gets home." Bobby turned, but he looked back over his shoulder. "I think you might be raising a lawyer."

"Anything is possible," she said and meant it.

# CHAPTER TWENTY

Life settled into a routine with Natalie opening the store and Jake bringing her coffee each morning. The town had taken a liking to Will and kept him busy while Natalie got used to the new routine.

Jake folded his paper and sat it on the table. "What about sports?"

Natalie pulled a stack of books from the latest delivery of boxes. "What about them?"

"I'm thinking about Will. He needs an outlet and a place to belong."

A deep crease formed between her eyes. "I never did sports."

He patted the table in hopes she'd come over and sit. When she pulled out the chair beside him, he reached for her hand.

"Did you ever want to be on a team?"

She pulled her bottom lip between her teeth. "Sure, but sports were expensive and not allowed."

He nodded. When he was a kid, he'd played hockey and lacrosse. Both were costly and could have put his parents into debt, but they knew how important it was to be a team player.

"That's true, but playing on a sports team gives him the opportunity to learn life skills like sharing, diplomacy, and patience."

"All right, what do you suggest?"

"Aspen Cove has started a little league of sorts. That could be a good place to begin."

His thumb slid over the soft skin of her hand. He missed touching her. Missed lying naked with her in bed. Even though Will knew they'd spent the night together, they weren't blatantly flaunting themselves in front of him.

With Will's upbringing, he didn't have a handle on what a relationship looked like. His father had women coming and going at all hours of the day and night. Jake wasn't sure coming and going was wise. It wouldn't teach him about restraint or respect.

"What do you say?"

"Who do I talk to about it?"

"Bowie and Cannon are organizing it. They also have an adult version. Care to join?"

Her shoulders shook with her laughter. "You know that kid who gets picked last on a team?" She pointed to herself. "Well, that's me. I can't throw a ball, hit a ball, or kick a ball, but I can be a good cheerleader."

He had a vision of her in a short skirt and pom-poms. "Care to show me your routine in private?"

She snorted. "Privacy? That's a thing of the past. Somehow, I went from a single thirty-year-old to parenting a twelve-year-old. I skipped all the stuff in between like dating and girls' nights out."

"You had opportunities. I know you did, but something tells me you passed on them."

She nodded. "I'm not all that great with people."

If only she could see herself the way he, and others, saw her. She wasn't unlovable or unlikable. She was resistant.

"You are, but you're not comfortable, so you avoid it. Being around people is like wearing a new pair of shoes or jeans straight from the dryer. It's not a comfortable fit until you break them in. Give it a chance, and if the fit isn't right, then you try something else on."

"Okay, Mr. Wise One. I don't see you hanging around anyone in town. Where are your friends?"

He pulled his hand back and stretched as if he were getting ready to list a thousand names from memory.

"I have friends. I hung out with Tilden, Cannon, and Bowie. I've played pool with Dalton. Doc and I enjoy a beer together occasionally. My best friend, Addis, and I talk twice a week."

"Addis? What's an Addis look like?"

He didn't know how to describe him, so he pulled up his picture. "He's the one hanging from the harness." Addis was a favorite with the ladies. He'd seen firsthand how many women threw themselves at him.

"Oh my God, that's you above him. You're a rock climber?"

Warmth filled him that she totally bypassed the rock-climbing GQ model and focused on him. "No, but I try new things. I didn't climb that rock. I took a copter to the top and repelled down it. Addis is the outdoorsman. I'm the wannabe."

"You jumped off a cliff with only a rope? Do you have a death wish?"

She sounded like his mom the day he posted his pictures to social media.

"No, I have a life wish. This was a year after my surgery. I had a bucket list of things I wanted to do. That picture was taken the same year I wrote *Love the Life You Live*."

"That makes you a great life coach. You practice what you preach."

"Life is about taking risks. If there's no risk, there's no reward. Whether or not you believe it, you're a risk-taker too." He leaned forward and waited for her to meet him in the middle. "You took a risk on Will, Aspen Cove, and you took the biggest risk on me." It probably wasn't good to point things out. "Little by little, you're opening your heart to new possibilities."

"Maybe, but it's more like I'm being pushed into the deep end, and I've learned how to tread water."

He gently touched his lips to hers. "I'm happy to be your lifeline."

"You're too risky. That only means I'll drown when you leave because there's no one there to help keep me afloat."

He'd lost that battle, but he still had a chance of winning the war. Natalie was opening herself up to new possibilities.

He scooted his chair back and rose. "I'm going to visit my friend Bowie and find out when Will can start."

She jumped up and followed him to the door. "What if I can't afford it?"

He gave her ponytail a swift yank. "You can. I know how much you make, but if you couldn't, I'd take care of it. You know ... why not offer an Aspen Cove Athletic Scholarship?"

"You're impossible."

"Yes," he said as he walked out the door. "But something tells me you love it."

She waved her hand dismissively. "You and your love."

---

JAKE PLAYED right field with Will. He couldn't believe the kid had never picked up a baseball.

Cannon hit the pitch, sending it straight toward them. "You got it?"

"Yes," Will said excitedly.

He held up his mitt and moved around, trying to figure out the exact place it would come down. He'd missed two before, so he needed this win to boost his confidence.

"You've got this."

"I got it."

It hit the mitt with a slap that sent Will back a few feet, and he opened it to find he really did have it.

"I have it. I really have it." He raised it into the air like a trophy. The joy on his face lit up the field. "Nat, I caught it," he yelled.

She was on her feet, whooping it up from the stands. "That's my brother right there," she yelled for his benefit.

Since the kids' team was comprised of mostly little ones, the adults let Will and Brian play with them. The teams divided between food service and everything else. Since Will was now associated with the bookstore, he was on the everything else team, whereas Dalton, Cannon, and Katie were part of the foodies. There weren't any dues to pay. The only expense was a pair of cleats and a mitt, and Jake bought those because that's what men did.

Will tossed the ball back to Bowie, who pitched for their team. "I can't believe I caught that."

Jake ruffled Will's hair. "You can do anything you put your mind to. You've already shown us that. Anytime someone tells you that you can't do something, if it's something you want badly, then prove them wrong."

Will dropped his glove and wrapped his arms around Jake, hugging him like both their lives depended on it.

"In case I forget to tell you, this is the second-best day of my life."

Jake leaned back to look at him. "What's the first?"

Will looked to the bleachers and waved to Natalie. "The day she came and got me, but I didn't know it then. I was certain I was heading straight to H E double hockey sticks, but this"—he looked around—"is as close to heaven as I've ever been."

Weeks ago, Will would have said hell and a bunch of other colorful words, but he was learning. "I'm glad it's working out for you."

"Finally, I have a family. Natalie is like the mom I never had, and you're ..." Will lowered his head. "You're the dad I wish I had."

Could his heart feel any fuller and not burst? "You'd be the perfect son, Will."

He laughed. "Don't forget, we're not supposed to lie. I'll never be perfect, but I'll try to be better."

"That's all we can ask."

An hour later, they sat in the diner, eating burgers and fries. Since the foodies lost, it was their treat. He wondered what the cost of a loss would be for the everything else team. Would Bowie have to hand out fishing poles and tackle? Would he have to give away books? He chuckled when he thought of what Aiden Cooper the sheriff would offer. Handcuffs for everyone? A get out of jail free card?

"What are you smiling about?" Natalie asked.

He wouldn't tell her cuffs and tackle, so he looked straight into her eyes and said, "Our next date." Will ran off to play with Brian, leaving them alone in the booth. "Since Louise invited Will to spend the night tomorrow, how about a sleepover at my place?"

She lifted a brow. "Your place?"

"Seems only fair since we had our first night at yours. I'll take care of everything. All you have to do is show up with an appetite."

She slicked her tongue across her lips. "What are you serving?"

"Anything you want."

He knew exactly what she wanted—a repeat of their first night together. They'd kissed and touched and teased, but they were never together long enough to get more than a taste. By the glint of fire in her eyes, he knew she was hungry.

"Bring a big appetite." He leaned in and whispered, "Clothes are optional."

# CHAPTER TWENTY-ONE

How did a person prepare for a sleepover? In all of her thirty years, she'd never been to one. She wasn't allowed to as a kid, and she never had a desire as an adult. Sleepovers implied intimacy. The kind two people shared when they were best friends or more than lovers.

"Will, don't forget your toothbrush." She grabbed hers and put it in her backpack before moving to stand in front of her dresser. She opened the drawer and groaned. There wasn't anything sexy or remotely attractive. White cotton hipsters were all she owned. They were sturdy and washed well.

"Jake didn't seem to care the last time," she said as she plucked a fresh pair from the drawer and dropped them into the bag.

"Will, clean underwear, too."

From across the hall, he groaned. The soles of his shoes thunked as he stomped across the wooden floor.

Inside she laughed. It was the simple things these days that thrilled her. The tiny upgrades in her life made a huge difference. Things like having spare change in the bottom of her purse and not knowing exactly how much was there because she didn't need to pinch pennies. The simple act of being able to use a full measure of laundry detergent or buying a loaf of bread from the grocery store instead of the day-old bakery.

Those were the things that tickled her. While the town provided the house and so much more, it was Jake who provided her job and endless kisses that filled her full to bursting with happiness. He made her feel wanted. Somehow, despite her meager existence, her cotton panties, and her general lack of everything, in his presence, she felt rich.

She spritzed on her dime-store body spray, picked up her tube of Chapstick, and walked into the living room.

"Are you ready?" she called to her brother.

"Coming."

She heard him race around his room to gather the stuff he wanted to share. Somehow, he'd gone from owning a few books to having his own collection of Legos, action figures, and games.

He tottered down the hallway with his arms full. When his prized GI Joe fell from the top, and he leaned over to catch it, the whole mountain of toys fell to the floor.

She dropped her bag and rushed over to help him pick up the treasures he hoped to share with the Williams kids.

"Are you sure you need all of this?"

He looked at the three boxes, two books, and four action figures lying on the wooden floor. "Yes, I do."

She laughed. "Last time you were there, an action figure ended up as Barbie's husband." She stacked the boxes, books, and boy dolls and placed them back in his arms. She knew Will wasn't showing off. She got it. He just wanted to fit in, and having things to share helped him achieve his goal. "Why don't we put those things in a bag?"

Ten minutes later, they were standing in front of Louise's door.

As soon as it opened, Will dashed inside.

"Hey, aren't you going to say goodbye?"

He blushed, tossed his head from side to side, and came back to give her a hug. "It's not like I'm moving out."

Louise looked at the overstuffed grocery bag. "Are you sure? By what you're bringing in, it appears you might stay forever."

Will laughed. "Would you even notice?"

Louise pointed down the hallway to where Brian waited in front of his room. "Get down the hallway, little critter." She turned to Natalie. "It would probably take me a few days to realize I had one more."

"Thanks for taking him."

Louise lifted a brow. "Are you having another date night with Mr. Sexy?"

Thinking about the night ahead, Natalie's insides turned warm and gooey. "Maybe," she said coolly. "He's making me dinner. Told me to bring an appetite."

Louise waggled her brows. "That doesn't mean he's cooking dinner."

She could feel the heat of the blush rush to her cheeks. "It doesn't mean he isn't."

With a wave of her hand, Louise dismissed her remark. "Honey, that man has it bad for you. I see it. Maisey sees it. Hell, the whole town sees it. Why can't you?"

"Oh, I know he likes me." She considered his feelings

for her. That night they first made love, he told her he could love her. But words said during passion weren't always true. It could be the voice of hormones fogging the brain. "I think I'm a nice distraction while he waits for his opportunity to open up." She lifted her shoulders in a shrug. "I might even be a project for him."

"I don't think so. I believe he genuinely cares about you. Whether you want to admit it, you care about him too. I see it in your eyes when you think no one is looking. Do you love him?"

Her question sent Natalie's heart racing. That built-in fight-or-flight response took over.

"This isn't about love. We're friends."

"With benefits." Louise looked behind her, and when she saw no one, she leaned in and asked, "Is he generous with those benefits? I mean ... a girl needs a solid employment package these days if you know what I'm getting at."

"Are you asking me if his package is solid or if it's comprehensive?" She giggled. "It's both."

"That makes him a keeper right there. Have you ever wondered why I have eight kids?" She rolled her shoulders. "It's because Bobby offered a solid and comprehensive benefits package too."

"I kind of jumped into the parenting role with both feet. If parents started with a pre-teen, there would be a lot of single-child homes."

"Nonsense. Every age is trying, but it's also rewarding. You missed out on the hours of rocking a baby in your arms. The first steps and words. You might raise Will, and you'll love him to the ends of the earth, but it's different when you look into the eyes of a child and see yours reflected back. You and Jake would make beautiful babies."

"There isn't a Jake and me. He's leaving."

"Are you sure? Seems to me, he's staying a lot longer than he planned."

The sigh she let loose settled in the air between them. "He's waiting for the offer."

Louise leaned against the doorjamb. "Did you know that Bobby was all ready to go into the Army? He was packed and prepared to head to the recruiter's office in Denver. They'd scheduled his physical and everything."

"Bobby was in the army?"

"No, that's my point. He jumped in his truck and got halfway to Denver when he decided I was all he needed. He came right back, rushed me to Copper Creek to get married, and took over his dad's garage. His parents moved to Texas, and the rest is history."

"That's so romantic."

"Or silly. I imagine he thinks about how different his life would be if he'd stayed the course and joined the army."

"It's obvious he made the right decision. All you have to do is see how he looks at you and the kids to know he loves you."

"He either loves me or knows that paying child support on eight kids would kill him."

A ruckus started down the hallway with the girls fighting over a doll.

"Looks like you're needed."

Louise glanced over her shoulder. "They'll figure it out. And you ... you will too. That man waiting for you more than likes you. Have fun. Don't worry. I'll call if Will needs to come home; otherwise, we'll see you tomorrow when you're ready to come get him."

Natalie wasn't affectionate by nature, but she reached

for Louise and gave her a hug. "Thank you for everything."

"No, thank you."

"By the way, Doc wants bigger pieces of pie."

The two women hugged again before Natalie left for Jake's. The entire ride up to the cabin, she let herself fantasize about what a life with Jake would look like. Marriage, babies, family dinners. It was right out of a movie. But the realist in her knew that all good movies had an end.

When she pulled in front of the cabin, she took a deep breath and tried to convince herself that she wasn't in love with Jake.

# CHAPTER TWENTY-TWO

He'd done everything in his power to create a romantic getaway for them. The cabin was a single room that contained everything they needed for the night. He'd set the table with a mish-mash of dishes and glasses. There were wildflowers in a mason jar in the center. He'd found several honey-scented candles on the shelf and placed them around the room to create ambiance.

Dinner was in the oven, and the smell of his favorite vegetarian lasagna filled the air. A bottle of cabernet sat breathing on the counter.

He took a final look around to make sure he was ready. Why this date seemed more important, he couldn't say, but it was. Inside he knew the truth, but he didn't want to admit it to himself. He was in love with Natalie Keane.

On paper, they were complete opposites. She was poor, and he was rich. She was closed off, and he was open. She didn't ask for much, and he wanted everything. But somehow, they were the perfect fit. She fed off his strength, and he settled into her acceptance. He bought things she couldn't afford, and she gave him things he could never buy. Somehow over the last few weeks, she'd become a necessity in his life.

He knew she considered him to be her savior, but the opposite was true. She'd shown him that he had more to offer than life advice. The scars that used to run deep were now superficial, and she kissed them like they were the best part of him.

He hated to admit it, but while he taught people how to navigate life, Natalie had shown him how to actually live.

The tires on the gravel told him she was here. The pace of his heart picked up. She wasn't even in the door, and yet his body filled with heat. It wasn't all passion. Most of it was a warm fuzzy feeling of being with the one person who made a difference in his existence.

He picked a piece of lint from the shoulder of his shirt —the blue shirt she loved the most—and made his way to the door. When he opened it, she was standing on the porch with a smile and her backpack.

Dressed in jeans and a soft aqua T-shirt, she was gorgeous.

"Come in." He stepped aside to let her pass. "You look beautiful, Natalie."

"Not so bad yourself." Her fingers ran across his chest as she passed him. "I love that shirt."

"I love …" He almost said *you*, but he didn't. "I love that you're here."

She glanced around the room that held everything from a kitchen to a bed to a living room all in one space.

"And I thought my tiny house was efficient. This place is …"

"Small," he said. He took her bag and tossed it on the

sofa before he wrapped his arms around her. "I missed you."

"You saw me earlier today in the bookstore."

He brushed his palm over her cheek. The soft strands of her hair caught between his fingers.

"You're like a Twix. They always put two in a package because one isn't enough." He kissed her softly, sensually, slowly.

When they finished the first kiss, she laid her head against his chest.

"Eat too many, and you'll get sick."

"I could never get sick of you." He walked her to the center of the room. "So this is it. Dinner will be ready in about thirty minutes. I thought we could enjoy a glass of wine and each other."

Her eyes went straight to the bed.

He hadn't put rose petals on it, but the sheets were clean, and he'd laid a single daisy on her pillow.

"What do you want first, the wine or the enjoyment?"

He chuckled. "I didn't expect that you'd arrive, and we'd jump straight into bed."

"But you wouldn't mind, right?" She pulled off her shirt and walked to the bed. "I mean ... whatever you're cooking smells great, but why waste thirty minutes chatting when we could build up an appetite?" She reached behind her and unclasped her bra. It fell to the floor next to her feet.

Natalie was naked from the waist up, asking if he'd rather chat or get on with enjoying her. Was that even a question?

"I told you to bring an appetite."

She kicked off her Keds and tugged at the button of her jeans. "I'm starving."

For a woman who didn't say too much or show her cards too easily, Natalie was laying down her hand tonight.

He crossed the room to where she stood and gazed into her eyes. "This isn't about sex."

She giggled. "Don't fool yourself. We both expected and wanted sex."

He couldn't argue. "True." He couldn't think straight when her hands were tugging his shirt up and over his head. "But it's more. This is about two people spending time together, getting to know one another more intimately."

She tossed his shirt to the side and started on the button of his jeans.

"Yes, and that means sex."

The denim fell from his hips; he kicked out of his shoes and pulled her onto the bed. She was naked, and he wore socks.

"It's more than sex, Natalie. It's—"

She cut him off with a kiss. "Let's start with this and figure the rest out later."

The next thirty minutes were filled with sensory overload. She touched his body without reservation. Her fingers tormented him. Her tongue tortured him. She made his heart sing, and his body crave more before they even finished. They lay beside each other with jelly legs and sweat covered bodies until the timer for dinner rang.

"You hungry?"

"For food?"

"You're insatiable."

He unfurled his body from hers and stood. Looking down at her pinkened skin, he could see where his kisses were too rough, and the scruff of his beard too abrasive, but the only word that came to mind wasn't *sorry*. It was *mine*.

He helped her up and, instead of handing her the shirt she'd arrived in, he gave her the blue one. Pulling it over her head, it settled around her thighs like a dress. He'd never seen anything look so sexy on a woman.

He rushed to the bathroom to clean up and came back to dress in his jeans and a fresh polo—the green one—her second favorite.

He pulled out her chair and poured her a glass of wine. Once he served up the lasagna, he took a seat across from her.

"This is my favorite meal."

She lifted a brow. "This?" The look was suggestive.

And when she glanced back at the bed, he laughed.

"Okay, my second favorite."

When she put the first bite into her mouth and moaned, he was a goner. All the sounds Natalie made were great, but the sound that came out of her mouth right then was like porn.

"Oh my God, you're the whole deal. You're sexy, good in bed, employed, and you can cook."

He took a bite and had to admit that it was amazing. "And I make tea."

"Yes, that's the most important aspect."

"Right, now hurry up and eat because I'm dying to have dessert." It was his turn to be suggestive, and his glance at the bed was not misinterpreted.

She wiggled in her chair. "I love dessert."

He kept it to himself, but inside he said, "and I love you."

# CHAPTER TWENTY-THREE

Her body ached in all the right places. Jake had made love to her in ways she could only dream about. It was more than the physical connection; something about him linked with her heart. He'd shown her what love could look like if the person she was with really cared.

"I wish we could stay here all day," Jake said, sitting in the corner of the room in the overstuffed chair. They'd started their morning with passion and ended it with oatmeal and email.

She tied her shoe and shoved her clothes into her backpack, including his blue shirt. He had put it on her, so now it was hers.

"Me too, but I need to get Will. It wouldn't be fair to leave him there much longer."

He rose from the chair and walked to her. "It's Sunday. How about a row on the lake and an ice cream? We'll pick up Will and can come back later to get your car."

Butterflies danced in her belly. She'd never had a

good look at what a healthy relationship looked like. If she had to guess, this was a prime-time ad.

"Really, you want to hang with us?"

He slid his body close, pressing his hips to hers. "I'd rather be in bed, but since that's not an option, ice cream seems like a good alternative."

"Sam's Scoops?"

"It's the only way to go."

Like the gentleman he was, he led her to his SUV and helped her inside. He kissed her so thoroughly she almost caved and called Louise to see if they'd keep Will another night, but she couldn't be selfish. Will would want ice cream and time with Jake too.

They made the drive down the mountain holding hands.

"Have you heard anything about the job?" Her heart twisted, thinking about it, but she'd rather prepare than have the news of his departure hit her like a bullet train when it happened.

"Nope. I'm thinking they might have changed their mind about me."

Deep inside, she hoped so, but if she were honest with herself, even if they'd changed their mind, it didn't mean he'd stay in Aspen Cove. He had a life in Phoenix.

"They'd be stupid not to want you."

"You can't always know what people think. There have been a lot of times when I thought someone wanted me, and I was wrong. There are lots of things to consider when making such a big decision."

She rolled those words around in her brain. The one thing she'd learned lately was that it wasn't things that needed consideration, but people.

"Do you think Jenny regrets leaving you?"

He turned and gave her a sideways look. "What made you think of Jenny?"

She situated herself, so her leg was bent on the seat, and she faced him as much as the seatbelt would allow.

"Just thinking about how we make choices. She expected you to die, and you didn't. Her choice meant she had to live without you. That must feel like a loss." Before he could say anything, she continued. "Like me. I took in Will, and that choice means that I'm responsible for him forever. I never considered that when I drove down to Los Angeles."

"Do you regret taking in Will?"

"No," she said a little too vehemently. "I'd do it all again, but what I'm getting at is the choices we make have everlasting effects on our lives."

"It's true. As for Jenny, I think she made the right choice, and it was a gift to me too. Anyone who can leave me when I need them the most isn't the person I want to be with."

He turned on to the highway and headed toward town.

"Thanks for a great night."

He reached over and placed his hand on her knee. "Natalie, the time I spend with you is some of the best moments of my life. You fill me full of ..."

He seemed to struggle for words. "This morning, it was oatmeal."

He nodded. "Yes, but last night it was happiness and hope."

They were only a few blocks from Louise's. She'd texted before they left to let her know they were on their way so Will could be ready.

"Is it hard to be in that cabin when you have such a great place in Phoenix?"

He turned on to the street and inched toward the house. "Who says my place is great?"

"It has to be. It's the penthouse, and you had a designer decorate it."

He parked the car but did not try to get out. "It's a house, not a home. It has all the things a person wants, but none of what I need."

He unbuckled and climbed out of the SUV.

As he rounded it to open her door, she asked herself, "What does a man like Jake Powers need?" Her mind answered for her. *Vision Quest.* He had money and power, and all the things he could desire. What Jake wanted most of all was the respect of his peers.

What she desired most was Jake.

---

WILL WAS up for ice cream and rowboats. The minute they pulled into the parking lot, he was out of the car and running to the Sam's Scoops truck.

"The life of a kid. His only worry is what flavor he's getting today." Jake helped her out, and they walked hand in hand to the truck.

The last time she was here with him, he carried her to the picnic bench, which now held a family of four.

"I'm glad his life will be good. At his age"—she shook her head—"I was cleaning houses for the neighbors for a meal."

"It never ceases to amaze me how much you went through and how incredibly solid you are as a human."

She leaned into him. "You know what they say ... What doesn't kill us strengthens us."

He tugged her closer and placed a kiss on top of her head. "They also say, why settle for one scoop when you can have two? What will it be?"

They ordered their ice creams. Will had a scoop of Pigeon Poop and one of Witch's Warts. She didn't even want to know what was in them. She chose Tar Pit, which was Sam's fancy name for rocky road. Jake erred on the side of caution, too, and had the same.

When they finished, they swung on the swings, slid down the slide, and made their way to the O'Grady's Equipment Rental.

"What will it be today?" a man named Seth asked from behind the counter. His eyes never took a glance at Jake or Will. The man was singularly focused on her, his flinty eyes eating her up like she was a bowl of Sam's sweet cream.

Jake cleared his throat. "We"—he pointed to himself, Will, and her—"would like a rowboat."

Seth snapped back like he'd been slapped. "Oh, you're together."

Will bounced on the balls of his feet. "Yep, we're together, like a family."

Seth's lips pinched, and he let out a grunt. "The pretty ones are always taken."

Jake slipped his arm around her waist. "This one is. She's mine."

Natalie's knees grew weak, and she nearly hit the floor, but over the years, she'd learned to recover well when things surprised her. Instead of setting things straight like she'd been doing all along, she tried it on for size.

"Yep, I'm his." Not to leave Will out, she patted his back and said, "and he's ours."

"Down the dock and second slip on the right. It's fourteen an hour or thirty for the day."

"We'll take it for the day," Jake said and wrapped his free arm around Will's shoulder and led them out.

It took a little practice, but once Will and Jake got in sync with each other, they were gliding across the mirrored surface of the lake. All she had to do was sit and enjoy.

They moved past a few fishermen who were more than happy to show off the day's catch to an eager boy.

"Can we go fishing sometime too?" Will asked.

"Absolutely, but you either have to catch and release or eat what you caught."

Will shivered. "I don't like fish unless they come deep-fried and in sticks."

"Then it's catch and release."

They made their way across the lake to the falls where some older kids were jumping from the cliff into the pool below.

"Can we do that too?" Will swished his fingers through the water. "Not today, but later in the summer when the water is warmer?"

"I'm not jumping off a cliff," Natalie said, then looked at Jake. The picture of him repelling came to mind. "That's totally in Jake's lane, but I'll visit you in the hospital when you're finished."

Jake sat across and locked eyes with her. "No risk ... no reward."

"Tell me that when you're in a body cast and I'm feeding you liquids through a straw."

"The hardest part is taking the leap." He stared at her,

and something told her they weren't talking about cliff diving.

"No sense in taking a leap at nothing."

He frowned and continued to row. They made their way back to the dock.

Before they could get out of the boat, Will flung himself into Jake's arms.

"Whoa, buddy, what's up?"

"Just wanted to let you know that this was the perfect day."

"Yes, rowing the boat was fun."

Will moved back, and a stern expression crossed his face. "No, it wasn't the boat ... I mean, that's part of it."

"Okay, what else made it perfect?" Jake asked.

Will looked between them. "I was with my family. I love you both and want every day to be like this."

Jake pulled Will in for a hug, but his eyes were on her. "I love you, too. Both of you."

Her heart nearly burst. He'd told her he could love her, but that was because they were naked. Today, they were fully clothed, and he said it anyway. He looked at her like he was waiting for the words to spill from her lips too. She opened her mouth to say them but couldn't. To say them meant it was real, and to make it real made it dangerous for her heart. Love was like Voldemort from Will's favorite book. It was the emotion that couldn't be called by name, otherwise, it would have power over her. Instead, she said, "I want a thousand more days like this."

His eyes dimmed before her, but he leaned in, crushing Will between them and said, "I'll give them to you."

# CHAPTER TWENTY-FOUR

He sat at the corner table, going through his emails while Will finished up his winding down session. Since Sunday, they'd spent every minute they could together, as a family, and it felt so damn right.

He pondered his luck and wondered if maybe not hearing from Vision Quest wasn't bad. He'd come to Aspen Cove to pay a gift forward, and in return, he'd received an even bigger one. While Natalie wouldn't give him the words he so badly wanted to hear, she showed him her love in many ways.

Then there was Will, who was a kid who had never known what real love looked like and was getting a daily dose by his sister, the community, and him.

"The end," Will said and closed the book.

"Good job, Will," Natalie said, rounding the corner with a basket of heart-shaped I READ A BOOK TODAY stickers. "Don't forget your sticker and come back next week for ..." She pointed to Will.

"Oh, right. I've picked out a Berenstain Bear book

called *Pirate Adventure*." He stared at his sister. "Can we dress up like pirates?"

Natalie laughed. "Sure, if they want, but a costume isn't required."

As the kids left, talking excitedly about what they wanted to wear, his phone rang. When he saw the caller was Vision Quest, it filled him with both excitement and dread.

He looked at Natalie. He got dozens of calls a day from clients, but her expression told him she somehow knew who this call was from.

He walked into the office and shut the door.

"Hello, Matt." He slid into the seat behind the desk. "I didn't think I would hear from you."

There was a moment of silence and a clearing of Matt's throat. "I'm sorry. Things took longer than we had hoped. We interviewed Fritz, and then the female members of the board asked why we hadn't considered Trudy Heinz or Sally Walters. That opened up an entirely new can of worms regarding the balance of power. I'm telling you, it's been a shit show."

"Did you find the right candidate for the job?" Somewhere deep inside, he hoped they had hired someone else, and this was the call to tell him he hadn't been chosen. That was the easy way out of this situation. If the decision had been made, then it would save him from making the hard ones for himself.

"It was always you."

He held back a laugh. Those were the words he wanted to hear, but not from Matt Steinman.

"That's not exactly true."

"Sure, it is, but we had to be certain. This is a big commitment from both sides."

"What was the deciding factor for choosing me?"

"Well, you have it all. Your skill set is unparalleled, you're likable, and you have deep pockets."

"Ah, yes, the deep pockets are important." He knew his financial stability was a plus, but he didn't want it to be the sole reason for their decision.

"When can you start?"

"That's a good question. I'll get back to you in a few days to iron things out." He hung up before Matt could press him for a more definitive answer. Weeks ago, he would have said tomorrow, but things had changed.

He leaned back in the chair and closed his eyes. He tried to imagine his future and the images that came up varied. The first being Natalie swinging at the park with her hair blowing in the wind. He saw Will as a teenager driving his first car, on his first date, and at graduation. He imagined a little girl running into his office and throwing her arms around his neck. Looking down, she had green eyes and hair as soft as her mother's. Thoughts of his office followed with pictures of Vision Quest and the walks he would take along the bluff looking over the Pacific Ocean. He saw the patients who would write and say their lives were better because he was in them. He wanted it all, but could he have it all?

A soft knock sounded at the door.

"Come in," he sat up and watched as Natalie entered. She left the door partially ajar so she could hear if a customer needed her help. She was the perfect pick for the job—not that he had many options, but he couldn't see anyone else behind that register, and that left him with another problem. If he left Aspen Cove, he would want to bring Natalie and Will with him, but who would run the store? He'd be back where he started.

She leaned against the wooden desk. There was pain in her eyes, she masked with a smile.

"Was that the call?" The last word came out in a squeak.

He scooted back and patted his lap, but she stayed where she was.

He scrubbed his face with his hands. "It was."

"That's great. I knew they would call." Her false sense of bravado both crushed him and warmed him.

"It's not a done deal."

She nodded. "Sure it is; that's what you wanted. I'm glad you got the job. It's important to you."

Will walked in at the mention of a job.

"What job?"

Natalie hopped off the desk and went to Will to pull him in for a hug. "Jake got his dream job. He'll be leaving us soon." She swallowed the knot in her throat.

Will fought to get out of her embrace. "He can't leave us; he loves us. People who really love you don't leave."

Jake stood. "Will—"

Natalie held up her hand. "I've got this." She gripped the boy's shoulder, so it forced him to look at her. "Love doesn't make people stay forever."

Will broke free and took off toward the front door.

Jake rushed after him. "I'll get him."

She grabbed him. "No, I know what he's feeling, and he needs time to process. Let him be."

"Natalie." He turned toward her and opened his arms. This time she stepped into them. Her body shook next to his, but she didn't make a sound, and she didn't shed a tear. "I love you. Come with me to California."

She drew in a jagged breath and stepped back. "I

can't. This is where I belong. This is where Will belongs. Aspen Cove is home."

"Then I'll stay. Just say the word, and I'll stay."

She stared at him for several minutes. "That sounds so easy, but it's not. You'd stay because of guilt, and I'd hate myself for it."

"I'd stay if you just told me how you feel."

She took a deep breath. "I feel like it's time for you to go." She walked past him and turned left into the non-fiction aisle to stock books.

"Natalie, please."

She turned, and he saw the tears falling freely down her cheeks. "Go, Jake. It's what I want, and what you need." Her back was to him.

He walked out of the bookstore, intent on finding Will, but found himself in the diner sitting in front of Doc putting his heart on the table.

"Do you love her?"

Jake thought long and hard about that question. He was certain what he felt was love.

"Yes. I love her."

"And the boy?"

"Him too."

"Now listen here, son, you have decisions to make, and they're hard ones. But before you do, let me tell you a story."

Doc waved Riley over for another cup of coffee and a big slice of apple pie. Once she arrived with coffee, pie, and a cup of tea for Jake, Doc began.

"Before my Agatha, I married Phyllis." His eyes soft-ened when he said her name. "She was my first love. I was smitten over that girl. I even killed my prize hog for her, but that's another story for a different day. The one you need to hear is this. I'm a doctor. I had scholarships to the best medical schools in the country. Harvard School of Medicine was at the top of my list."

"Is that where you went?"

Doc frowned and shook his head. "No, now listen, and don't interrupt because I'm old, and I might forget what I want to tell you."

"Okay, go on." He sat back and sipped his tea.

"Harvard had everything. It had the best facility. It had a reputation of excellence. I knew if I went there, the world would be my oyster, but you know what it didn't have?"

Jake opened his mouth to speak, but Doc shook his head.

"It didn't have my Phyllis. I could be a doctor anywhere, but I could only have Phyllis here in Aspen Cove."

"Are you telling me to stay?"

Doc grumbled to himself. "No, I'm telling you that sometimes you have to decide what's more important. For me, the choice was a Harvard education or the first love of my life. It wasn't a choice at all. Boulder was a fine school too. For you, it's different. All I'm saying is you came here for a reason."

Jake nodded. "Yes, to give back. To open the bookstore."

"Puppy brains," Doc said. "The town could do without a bookstore, but can you do without Natalie and Will? We didn't absolutely need a bookstore, but do Natalie and Will need you? Do you need them?"

# CHAPTER TWENTY-FIVE

Natalie waited for an hour for Will to return. She paced the aisles of the bookstore and cried. When her eyes hurt too much to see, and her head pounded so hard she couldn't think, she flipped the sign to closed and left. She was the manager, and Jake told her she could leave when important things came up, and Will missing fit that category.

She hopped into her old Subaru and drove to Hope Park first. Will loved to go there, and she thought maybe she'd find him on the swing set or the jungle gym, but the only people present were Charlie and Eden walking their strollers around the track.

Next, she stopped at the house, but it was silent and empty. A lump of fear lodged in her throat. Not only the panic of not finding Will but the dread of losing Jake.

She fell on the sofa and fisted her hands in her lap. A yell of frustration bubbled up, and before she could let it loose, her phone rang.

She dug through her bag to find it and noticed the caller was Louise.

"Hello." She hardly recognized her voice. It was small and childlike.

"He's here. I've made him some hot cocoa and hugged him for a bit. I thought you'd be worried sick, so I called."

"Thank you. I've been searching for him. I'll be right over."

"Wait. What about you? Are you okay?"

"I'll survive." She hung up and fell back to the cushions to take a breath. Relief washed over her. "It will be okay." That's what she'd tell herself until it was.

She teetered between devastation and agitation. The only person she could be angry at was herself. It would be so easy to rail against Jake, but what was the point? She knew what she was getting into when she jumped; she just didn't think she'd land so hard or painfully.

She rocked forward and stood. As she moved to the front door, she cried again.

---

TEN MINUTES LATER, she was on the front porch of Louise's house. The door swung open on her first knock.

Louise didn't say a word. She looked at her tear-stained face and tugged her in for a hug. "Oh, honey, it will be okay."

She sucked in a choppy breath. "I know, but it doesn't make it any easier."

Louise stepped back. "Will's playing with Brian and Eric. Kids are resilient. At least they can keep him focused on something else for a bit." She threaded her arm through Natalie's and led her to the kitchen. "It's almost five and time for wine."

Natalie didn't argue; she followed Louise and sat at the table that could serve an army.

"Our houses aren't anything alike."

"They used to be until I grew out of mine. It's a good thing Bobby is handy, and he's friends with Wes; otherwise, I'd be feeding my brood in shifts."

She poured two glasses of prosecco and handed one to Natalie. The first sip made her shudder. She preferred her wine dry and tart, but right now, she'd settle for anything that could numb her feelings.

"I finally fell in love, and now he's leaving." It was a thought she said out loud, and it surprised her how much lighter she felt letting the truth out.

"Does he know?"

She shook her head. "I've never said the words, though he's said them to me and to Will. Why would he tell us he loves us?"

"Because he does."

Louise grabbed a plate of cookies and set them on the table in front of Natalie. Prosecco was a dessert wine, but even she knew that wasn't supposed to be taken literally. Despite the sugar overload, she picked up a chocolate chip cookie and took a bite. She chewed it and washed it down with wine.

"Why do all the men in my life leave?"

"He's not gone yet. Convince him to stay."

"I won't ask him to give up his dream."

"Are you sure that's his dream?"

"He only came here to open the store because he's a big believer in Karma and felt the need to give back. If he could have found a manager for the bookstore right away, he would have left weeks ago. In fact, he almost lost the opportunity to run this fancy program in California because it took too long to convince me to come on board." She closed her eyes and ran her hand over her face. "I knew I shouldn't have let him in. I knew it, but for just a minute, I wanted something more."

Louise lined up three cookies, one chocolate chip, one sugar, and one peanut butter. She eeny, meeny, miny, moe'd them until she chose the sugar cookie.

"I see it differently. Consider this." She broke the cookie in two and dipped one half in her wine before she took the bite. She shuddered and made a face. "Not the same as milk." She pushed the wine and cookies away. "What if that was his original plan, but you changed everything?"

"He asked me to come with him."

Louise sat up. "See, he's not leaving you. He wants you and Will. If you love him, go with him."

"I can't. I have Will to consider. He's had enough uncertainty in his life. He's happy here. He has friends and a community that cares about him. I won't upset his new balance."

By the slow shake of her head, Natalie knew that Louise understood. "Ask him to stay."

"I can't. I won't. When Bobby drove away to join the army, did you ask?"

She smiled. "No, because I knew if I did, and his life turned out to be awful here, he'd always blame me."

There it was—the truth. She'd never put Jake in a position where he had to choose. Ultimatums didn't work out for anyone.

"I want him to stay because he wants to stay, not because he feels like he has to."

"That's fine, but don't choose for him either. That's just the ultimatum turned on its head."

"What am I supposed to do?" She didn't want Jake to leave, but she refused to ask him to stay. She felt like she was stuck between a rock and a wall.

"Love him while he's here. Let him go. If he comes back, it's not because you asked him to, but because he wanted to."

Natalie choked down the rest of the glass of wine and gathered Will. She had so much to think about. "Thank you, Louise, you've been so kind."

"We're friends, Natalie. Friends help friends and serve them shit wine."

Despite the situation, that brought a smile to her face. "I've never had a friend." That shook her.

"You've had lots of friends. There's a whole town that would consider you a friend or a friend in waiting. Let them in, and in the meantime, Jake is your friend, and if he's leaving, wouldn't it be nice to have more time with your best friend?"

As she and Will walked to the car, she considered Louise's counsel. Jake leaving didn't take him completely out of her life; it simply reverted him from lover to friend.

"How about we go for pizza in Copper Creek? If Jake's not busy, he can join us."

Will sat in the front seat with crossed arms and a frown. "Why would we invite him?"

How did she explain to a kid what she had a hard time processing as an adult? "Because he's our friend."

She sent a quick text to him.

**Heading out to Piper's for pizza. Care to join us? We could celebrate your good news.**

He wrote back right away.

**I'll be there.**

She beat him to the restaurant and waited in the same booth that they'd sat at before. Will headed straight to the arcade with a ten-dollar bill.

Each time the door opened, her heart raced. Each time it wasn't him, it sank.

When he appeared, her heart hurt. The sadness in his eyes was crushing. Jake was a positive person. She couldn't recall a single time where he appeared broken until now.

As his eyes adjusted to the dim lighting, he looked around until he saw her and rushed her way.

She would have slid out of the booth if she wasn't certain her knees would collapse. Instead, she moved over so he could sit beside her.

They both started with hi.

"You first," he said.

The *thump, thump* of her heart, drowned out the noise surrounding them. Gone was the radio, the chatter, and the pings and dings of games in the arcade. She was alone with him in a sea of sound and people she couldn't see or hear.

"Hi." She forced a smile to her face and prayed that the tears pooling in her eyes wouldn't spill forth. "Thanks for coming."

"I'll always be there for you."

*Wouldn't that be great?* "I'm sorry I got so upset. It's hard to lose someone you ... you care about."

He scooted closer. "You're not losing me."

"I know. We'll always be friends."

He took a deep breath in and let it out through his mouth. "This is not what I had imagined. I didn't expect to meet you and fall so hard and fast. I'll stay. All you have to do is ask."

She knew that was true. "I'd never ask. And before you tell me anything else, you need to know that this isn't me protecting myself from hurt. It's me protecting what we have, which is a wonderful friendship."

"But we're more than that." He cupped her cheek, and she leaned into his hand.

"Yes, we are."

"Come with me, Natalie. I can take care of you and Will. I want you in my life."

"I appreciate that, but I'm a girl who used to run from place to place looking for home, and I found it in Aspen Cove. I know you'd make Los Angeles great for us, but I won't take Will back to the place where he knew so much pain. You have a job to do. People need you." She leaned into him and rested her head on his shoulder. "You judge your worth in the world by how many people you can help, and you help so many. Look at what you did for us. Our lives changed because of you. Aspen Cove was my salvation, and I don't want it to become your hell."

Will walked to the booth with eyes full of distrust.

"Hey, buddy." Jake reached out to ruffle Will's hair, but Will sidestepped his touch.

"I thought you loved us," Will said.

Jake looked at Natalie. "I do. I love both of you."

"Nat says you're our friend, but you're breaking the rules." A tear slid from Will's cheek.

"What rule?"

"No cheating, no stealing, no lies."

"And which one did I break?"

"You stole our hearts, and you're leaving, which means you're stealing my hopes. I wanted you to be my family. You talk about living your life, but you don't practice what you preach. You let your life live you."

Jake stood and pulled Will into his arms. "I'm sorry, Will. I'm so sorry, but your sister is right. I have to do this. If I don't, then I'll never know and always wonder. As for family, you are family. The family I choose, and I'll always be there for you."

"Yeah, that's what they all say."

The next hour was more painful than the first because they remained silent. Any talk about the future or the past ended in tears.

Natalie had the waiter box up the pizza they didn't eat, and they walked out. She held on to him for a long minute before she raised on tiptoes to kiss him goodbye.

"You're the best man I know, Jake Powers. Stay that way." She climbed into her car and drove off.

# CHAPTER TWENTY-SIX

He stepped off the plane in Los Angeles. The airport was full of people rushing in every direction, but it appeared as if they weren't going anywhere. He grabbed his bag and made his way outside, where a car waited.

The day was warm though the sun didn't peek through the polluted sky. He'd heard the locals called it June gloom. While everywhere else was moving into summer, Los Angeles spent a month in a haze.

Up ahead, a man held a sign with his name. *Jake Powers,* it said. There was a time in his life that he'd have puffed up with pride seeing his name on display. Now he wondered if it really mattered. Notoriety didn't make life special; it only made life busy and complicated.

He'd driven by the bookstore on his way out of town, but Natalie had closed it for the day. He went by the house, but she wasn't there either.

He left Aspen Cove feeling hollower than the day he got his diagnosis. Back then, he was dying from an ailment. Today, he was succumbing to heartache.

"Are you Jake?" the rotund man dressed in a black suit asked.

"I am."

"I'm Roger." He took his bag and placed it in the back of the town car, and opened the rear door. "It's a twenty-minute trip if we had wings, but we have to get on the 405, and that means we'll travel like a slug. Welcome to your new home." He eased into the traffic, and they were on their way.

He thought about Natalie and how she didn't want to leave Aspen Cove because it was home. He thought about Doc and his story about Phyllis. Doc never left Aspen Cove because Phyllis was home. When was the last time he felt like anyplace or anyone was home?

"Yesterday," he said aloud.

"Excuse me?"

*Just thinking.* "Tell me, Roger, do you have a family?"

The man chuckled. "Three families. Two ex-wives and seven kids between them. The new wife hasn't left me yet, things are good, but she will."

Jake was taken aback. "Why would you say that?"

"I work too much. Do you know how many hours I have to work to pay child support and alimony? The first wife left because I didn't work enough, the second because I worked too much. Wife three, she'll figure it out. I spend more time making a living than I do having a life. Why does everything have to be so complicated?"

"It doesn't have to be." The words tasted bitter on his tongue. "It doesn't have to be," he repeated. "Holy hell, it doesn't have to be. Who am I trying to impress? Myself. What do I want in life? To be happy. Where am I happy? There. With her."

"You okay?"

Jake laughed. "Yes, I'm great." He threw his hands in the air. "Holy hell, I am great, but you're heading in the wrong direction." He would have stayed in Aspen Cove if she'd only told him she loved him. Now in hindsight, he wanted to smack himself upside the head. Those words were hard for Natalie because she expected him to leave —she knew he would, and he did. But she didn't have to say the words for him to know she felt love. She showed it when she let him go. She wasn't selfish in any way. She sacrificed her heart so he could achieve his dream. Looking out the window, he knew this wasn't the dream. He wanted clean air, Will's laughter, and her smile. Like Will said, wasn't it time he practiced what he preached? He could make a life or make a living. He chose life.

"Nope," Roger said. "I know where I'm going."

Jake leaned forward. "So do I, and it's not Vision Quest. Take me back to the airport."

"Listen, man, if I don't deliver you, I don't get paid."

"I'll pay you double. Take me back now."

"You got it." Roger whipped the car around and dropped him off in front of the terminal a few minutes later.

As he approached the counter, his phone pinged with an incoming message. It was Natalie.

**Hey, just making sure you arrived safely. Will and I miss you already.**

Did he tell her he was coming back? No, he'd keep that as a surprise.

**I just landed, and I'm on my way to where I need to be.**

He watched the dots scroll, then disappear and then scroll and disappear before she replied.

**I'm glad it's working out. Take care.**

His fingers danced across the keys. **It will work out, and I'll be back to see you and Will before you know it.**

He smiled as he approached the counter. "How fast can you get me to Denver?"

# CHAPTER TWENTY-SEVEN

The bookstore wasn't the same without Jake. It could have been because he wasn't around every corner to give her a kiss, a hug, or tell her how fabulous she was. Mostly it felt as if the sun forgot to rise today.

"Will, can you go to the diner and get us dinner to go? I don't feel like cooking."

He sprawled across a beanbag chair, doing a lot of nothing. "We have leftover pizza."

"I know, but that reminds me of Jake. How about burgers and fries?"

The mention of burgers and fries always cheered him up. "Are we rich?" He rolled off the bag and climbed to his feet.

She thought about the question for a minute. Jake once said there were different ways to measure wealth, and he was right.

"Yes, we are. We're rich in love and friendship and patience."

"But not money."

She shrugged. "It's all perspective. There will always be someone who has more, and someone who has less."

He rolled his eyes. "Now you sound like Jake."

She laughed. "I guess I do. He taught us a lot while he was here. He showed me I could trust others, and I could open my heart to love."

"Did you tell him you loved him?"

She shook her head. "No, I didn't."

He huffed and frowned. "Do you think he would have stayed if you had?"

She knew the answer. "Yes. I'm sure he would have."

Will stomped his foot. "Then why didn't you?" he yelled. "You're the reason he left."

"I loved him so much that I had to let him go, Will." As much as it hurt, it was the right decision. If he ever came back, it would be because he wanted to, not because he felt obligated.

"I don't get it."

She took a twenty from her wallet. "Someday you will, because you're smart, but for now get us burgers and fries. I'll close up. I added the Disney channel to our cable. How about we sit on the couch and watch movies?" The light twinkled in his eyes, but he'd never give in that easily.

"All right," he said with a sigh. "But no girlie love stuff."

She laughed.

She closed up the shop and walked by the self-help aisle to pull out his book. She'd done that at least six times that day just to look at his face. Rather than put it back, she tucked it inside her bag and left. Will was already in the Subaru eating his fries when she got in the car.

"Hey, I thought we would sit around and watch a movie while we ate, but you'll finish before we get home."

"Well, I saw Louise, and she asked me to stay the night. I said yes because I knew you wouldn't mind."

"Will, that's called manipulation, and it's a bad trait."

"Can I go anyway?"

She couldn't say no. Keeping Will happy and occupied kept him from moping around about Jake's absence.

"Yes, but next time you try to manipulate the situation, it will be a no. I'm letting you go this time because I know you're sad, and having friends makes you happy."

"Thank you, but you're sad too. What will you do?"

She wasn't about to tell him that she'd stare at the book and cry all night. Instead, she lifted her brows. "I'm watching Cinderella on repeat all night long."

Will made a gagging sound before digging into more fries.

She started the car and pulled out from behind the building. The sun set on the horizon, painting an orange glow across the sky. It was a perfect Aspen Cove day minus Jake.

She pulled into her driveway and glanced to her left to see the flowers blooming in her yard. Little by little, everything was coming together. She might not have love in her life, but she had everything else.

"Let's get inside so you can pack a bag." Will got out of the car and walked up the steps, stopping halfway. He turned toward her with a look of confusion. She hurried forward to see what was happening. Sitting on the porch looking exhausted but so damn sexy was Jake.

"Oh my God, what are you doing here?"

"I left my heart here, and I can't live without it."

Will didn't wait for explanations. He lunged forward

and nearly tackled Jake to the wooden planks. "I knew you'd come back."

Jake hugged Will and stood. "You did?"

Will nodded. "I did. You love us, and we love you. We belong together."

Jake stood and looked at her. "Yes, I love you, and I know you love me."

She moved toward him. "I do. I love you." She lifted on tiptoes and kissed him.

"Gross," Will said.

"You think that now but give it a year or two." Jake locked eyes with her. "I'm here to stay if you'll have me. I don't want to make a living. I want to make a life with you and Will. You are home to me. We're a family."

All the heaviness in her heart lifted. "Yes, we are."

A car pulled up in front, and Louise got out. "Are you ready, Will?"

He looked at Jake. "You're staying, right? Like when I get home tomorrow, you'll be here?"

He nodded. "Yep, I'll be here tomorrow and the next day and the next." He turned to Natalie. "If you'll have me."

"Are you crazy? I'll have you now and forever."

Will took the keys from his sister and unlocked the door. "Can I be the best man at your wedding?"

Natalie laughed. "Don't rush things, Will."

"Rush? I've been waiting all my life to have a family." He ran inside to get his things.

Louise walked up the sidewalk. "Perfect timing."

"Thanks, Louise. I appreciate it," Jake said.

Natalie narrowed her eyes. "You knew he was coming back?"

"Honey, they always come back."

Jake hugged Natalie to his side. "I called her from the road. I thought you might like to start the rest of our lives off right." He leaned down and whispered in her ear, "Naked and in my arms."

"Will, hurry up," she called. "My life is waiting for me."

He ran out with his backpack. He gave them both a hug, and just before he climbed into Louise's car, he yelled, "My room is still off-limits."

Jake picked up his suitcase and carried it inside. "I was thinking ... how do you want to do this?"

She cocked her head to the side. "Do what?"

He took her into his arms and held her tightly. "I'm thirty-six and not getting any younger. I don't want to waste a minute of my forever. I want marriage and a big family. I can have a ring on your finger by tomorrow, and a baby in your belly by next week. Does that work?"

She stepped back with a grin as wide as a canyon. "How about you put that baby in my belly tonight, and we get hitched at the courthouse tomorrow?"

She led him into their room, where they made love for hours. In the afterglow, she snuggled into his side and thought about her life. Abandoned by both her mother and father, she'd never been wanted or valued. She was afraid of the word love, but Jake showed her that love wasn't only a word, it was an action, an emotion, and a way of life, and she wondered how she'd ever survived without it. Her life was full, her heart was bursting, and all because a man came to town to give back. In the process, he gave her everything.

Next up is One Hundred Glances

OTHER BOOKS BY KELLY COLLINS

**Recipes for Love**

*A Tablespoon of Temptation*

*A Pinch of Passion*

*A Dash of Desire*

*A Cup of Compassion*

*A Dollop of Delight*

*A Layer of Love*

*Recipe for Love Collection 1-3*

**The Second Chance Series**

*Set Free*

*Set Aside*

*Set in Stone*

*Set Up*

*Set on You*

The Second Chance Series Box Set

**A Pure Decadence Series**

*Yours to Have*

*Yours to Conquer*

*Yours to Protect*

*A Pure Decadence Collection*

**Wilde Love Series**

*Betting On Him*

*Betting On Her*

*Betting On Us*

*A Wilde Love Collection*

**The Boys of Fury Series**

*Redeeming Ryker*

*Saving Silas*

*Delivering Decker*

*The Boys of Fury Boxset*

**Making the Grade Series**

*The Dean's List*

*Honor Roll*

*The Learning Curve*

Making the Grade Box Set

**Stand Alone Billionaire Novels**

*Dream Maker*

# JOIN MY READER'S CLUB AND GET A FREE BOOK.

Go to www.authorkellycollins.com

# ABOUT THE AUTHOR

International bestselling author of more than thirty novels, Kelly Collins writes with the intention of keeping love alive. Always a romantic, she blends real-life events with her vivid imagination to create characters and stories that lovers of contemporary romance, new adult, and romantic suspense will return to again and again.

*For More Information*
www.authorkellycollins.com
kelly@authorkellycollins.com

Printed in Great Britain
by Amazon